DEAD ON ARRIVAL . . .

She was a Chinese princess—dead for twenty centuries—a museum exhibit traveling through the Orient and trailing a wake of brand new murder!

Hidden somewhere in her death garment of precious stone was a microfilm with information more valuable than twenty nuclear secrets!

Killmaster's assignment: Get the film. Get it at any cost! When he arrived in Hong Kong, he found AXE agent N6 already dead and AXE's most valuable local contact butchered, Cantonese style.

The "jade princess" had started an undercover war, and Nick Carter was marked as the next victim!

THE NICK CARTER

KILLMASTER SERIES

Dedicated to The Men of the
Secret Services of the
United States of America

NICK CARTER

A Killmaster Spy Chiller

THE LIST

AWARD BOOKS
NEW YORK

FIRST AWARD PRINTING 1976

CHAPTER ONE

You couldn't see Red China, but you could sure as hell feel it. Outside Mao's showplace department store, Chinese Arts and Crafts, the walls were covered with oversized propaganda slogans and smiling beneficent portraits of the leader of the Cultural Revolution. Most of the pedestrians who hurried along Canton Road seemed oblivious to the luridly scrawled texts. It was just part of the changing scenery, the local color, the atmosphere of honky-tonk which makes Hong Kong so unique and such a favorite among travelers and tourists.

As far as I was concerned, the city made New York look like Boise, Idaho. You could hardly walk without bumping into people, without finding your gaze diverted by an unending variety of luscious-looking Chinese chicks—one of the many delights of the city.

But I wasn't feeling too delighted that particular morning. I had business to attend to—business that wasn't of a very casual or uncomplicated nature, either. Turning off Canton Road, I slipped into a side street and came out on Kowloon's main thoroughfare, Nathan Road. It was Macy's and Gimbels for one Golden Mile, as they call the major shopping area. Kowloon is the largest city on the mainland side of the crown colony. It was here, up above the strip of bustling shops and girlie bars, that I had an appointment with a man who didn't like to be kept waiting.

His name was Poy Chu. According to the file I'd read

back at AXE's Washington headquarters, he was reputed to be the most notorious Chinese double-agent currently around ... alive and kicking, that is. There had been scores of other greedy and ambitious men before him, but most of his predecessors had long since left this world for another. Poy Chu, however, seemed to have outlived them all. At the ripe old age of thirty-four, he had already made quite a name for himself and had a reputation for selling information that was top secret and of the highest quality.

It was precisely this kind of material I was after. I was prepared to pay the price, too, because Hawk had made it clear that Poy Chu's latest piece of information would send heads rolling in Peking once we got our hands on it. Somehow, the double-agent had managed to smuggle the goods out of Red China, though how he'd accomplished this near-miracle was something he hadn't told me. In fact, he hadn't told me very much of anything, save for the fact that I was to meet him at the most out-of-the-way spot he could think of: the Yue Lan—or Hungry Ghosts—Turkish Bath. It was one of Temple Street's numerous offerings—a hedonistic retreat sandwiched between a chop suey palace on one side and a bawdyhouse on the other.

Whatever negotiations were necessary, and I was sure they'd be considerable and time-consuming, would be conducted at the steam bath. When he'd gotten in touch with me at my hotel, I hadn't missed the note of urgency in his voice, that strange metallic ring of fear that told me there was very little time to lose. Maybe Poy Chu felt his number was coming up. Maybe the big boys in Peking had finally gotten wise to his double-dealing act. But whatever the reasons, Poy Chu didn't sound anything like his usual happy and confident self.

I made it to Temple Street on foot about fifteen minutes later. A cab would have taken much longer, considering the way traffic was backed up all the way down to the Star Ferry, at the foot of Nathan Road. Tourists were in short supply this far afield, but no one was paying me much mind as I hurried down the narrow and crowded little street which was a combination of New York's Lower East Side, Forty-second Street, and Chinatown all wrapped up in one gaudy and flashing neon package. Offered everything from porno pics to processed opium, I did my best to keep a low profile but if anyone was following me, he was doing a damn good job keeping himself out of the picture.

Number 27 Temple Street was a shabby, rundown tenement. The front door was locked from the inside and as I rang the bell I kept my eyes on the move in case I was attracting the attention I wanted to avoid, but none of the street people seemed particularly interested in my destination. Nevertheless, I found myself breathing a sigh of relief when the door was finally opened and I was admitted into the lair of the Hungry Ghosts. They were yet to make themselves known, though the woman who unlocked the door for me made her presence felt in ten seconds flat.

To call her striking wouldn't begin to do her justice. She was Suzie Wong revisited, dressed in a skintight sheath with a slit skirt that amply displayed her figure to its full advantage. And if her svelte lush body wasn't enough to claim your attention, she had a pair of come-hither eyes that grabbed you and kept on holding as if for dear life, whether you liked it or not.

I liked it.

She bowed low at the waist and motioned me forward with a hand whose long fingernails were lacquered a brilliant blood-red. At the far end of the narrow vestibule a beaded curtain led the way into the reception room. It was furnished in Massage Parlor Modern, a mixture of black velvet and red vinyl, with lots of foam rubber and imitation teak. Lounging on the numerous settees and couches were an assortment of China dolls of various shapes and sizes, each one more attractive and arousing than the other.

"You wish for full treatment with extras?" the madam asked, her hands on her hips and one leg cocked forward. Her slit skirt split even higher, revealing a smooth expanse of alabaster thigh—that and a little bit more, besides. "We have very clean girls."

She was doing her spiel, selling her stable like meat on the hoof. It was all prime, no doubt about it. In fact, if I hadn't had an appointment to keep, I wouldn't have even bargained with her. Whatever she was going to charge would have been worth it, beyond a shadow of a doubt.

"Do you have a steam room?"

She turned her lipsticked mouth down into a petulant frown. Obviously the use of that kind of facility was a hell of a lot cheaper than the more tactile pleasures she was trying to get me to buy. "No massage?" she asked. "No—" and she made a gesture with her hand, the interpretation of which is just about universal.

I shook my head. "Not today, but thanks all the same."

"This way, then," she said, about as annoyed as they come.

Sorry to be such a disappointment, I followed close behind. Another door, this one sheeted in metal, was opened at the far end of the reception room. The floor was covered with black and white tile and the odor of steam and sweat made me think of the gym at AXE headquarters.

"Attendant will give you locker key. Cost is eighteen dollars, Hong Kong," she went on. Then, even before I could say a word or nod my head, she looked at me and laughed. "Can you afford, big spender?"

Eighteen Hong Kong dollars is about three bucks American. "I'll splurge . . . just this once," I told her as the door swung shut behind me.

Poy Chu had said he'd meet me in the steam room, so I paid for the privilege, got a towel and a key, and went

off in search of my locker. Like the Dragon Lady's obscene gesture, the locker room was another universal constant. It looked just about the same as any back in the
States, with narrow wooden benches screwed into the
floor and rows of rusty white metal lockers.

No one was around when I took off my jacket and then
my shoulder holster. Wilhelmina would just have to go
into storage, at least for the time being. It was impossible
to conceal a Luger with just a towel around my waist. But
at least I had Pierre, my gas bomb, attached to my upper
thigh. Not that I'd need it, but you never can tell, especially in my business. As for my chamois-sheathed
stiletto, good old trusted Hugo, he too would have to be
relegated to the locker, whether I liked it or not. But
somehow I just didn't think Poy Chu would try to pull a
fast one. After all, I was the man with the bread, the hard
cash on the line. He, in turn, had something he wanted to
sell, and one just doesn't go out of his way to murder a
customer.

So I wasn't particularly worried about having to defend
myself. In fact, the only thing that did worry me was that
Poy Chu wouldn't accept the offer I was prepared to
make. Two hundred thousand dollars is a pretty big pile
of mad money. But the information he had to sell was
worth much more than that. And if anyone knew how
priceless it was, it was certainly Poy Chu. Still, there was
no sense double-guessing the man. I'd just have to play
everything by ear and hope he was hungry enough to
snap up my offer. If he wasn't . . . well, I'd worry about it
when the time came.

I finished getting undressed, stowed my clothes in the
locker and wrapped a scratchy white towel around my
waist. Then I locked up and secured the key around my
ankle with its elastic band. It made a nice cheery sound as
I headed towards the steam room. Now if things went as
happily as the sound of the key doing jingle bells as it

bounced up and down against my ankle, I'd be in terrific shape.

The minute I opened the heavy glass and steel door which led into the steam room, I got a sampling of what hell was like. The steam was so thick, you couldn't see where to place your feet. Dense clouds of it were heating up the close tight air so that I felt as if I was starting to simmer and turn red, just like a lobster in a pot. Rivulets of sweat began to stream down my chest, beads of perspiration dripped down my forehead into my eyes.

I swept my hand in front of my face and gave my eyes time to get used to the near absence of light. The place wasn't as pitch-black as it seemed upon entering and a minute or two later I could see sufficiently in front of me to make it across the hot cement floor without colliding into a bench or a wet and torpid customer. There were plenty of the former, ringing the rectangularly-shaped room. As for the latter, I had a feeling they were all following the Dragon Lady's advice and taking advantage of her bargain massage rates, with or without extras. That was fine with me, because now Poy Chu and I would have all the privacy we needed to conduct our delicate negotiations.

For a moment I thought I was early, because I didn't see anyone on the benches soaking up the steam. "Poy Chu?" I called out, my voice emerging wet and breathy as I tried to pierce the shadows and find the double-agent. When he didn't answer I climbed up onto one of the wooden benches and took another look around.

That's when I saw him.

He was stretched out on one of the benches to my right, looking for all the world like the heat had gotten to him. How he could sleep with the temperature nudging the mercury up to 120 was completely beyond me. Well, I thought, each to his own. A rude awakening wasn't on the agenda, but it just couldn't be helped. I climbed across the benches until I reached him, tapped him lightly on the shoulder and waited for him to wake up.

But the double-agent was apparently a very sound sleeper. "Poy Chu," I said again, louder than before. "Come on, ole buddy. We've got business to attend to." I shook him more vigorously and thought I heard him groan, but it was only the wooden bench creaking under my weight. Hot air rises, so the steam was twice as thick at the top of the tier of benches than it was near the floor and I could barely see him. His head was turned away from me, facing the dripping tile wall. "Hey, up and at 'em, guy," I said, taking his head in my hands and feeling the sweat streaming off him.

But no, it wasn't sweat. It was too thick, too sticky for perspiration.

I looked more closely, and saw my fingers stained a bright crimson. They were coated with blood and involuntarily I stepped back. "What the—" I said aloud. I turned his head in my direction and bent forward, trying to get a good look at him. His lips were curled back in a grimace of pain, surprise and rigor mortis. His eyes bulged out of their sockets—dead fish eyes that stared back at me, cold and lifeless.

Poy Chu's throat was neatly cut, from one ear to the other.

Most of the blood had already congealed, but there was enough of it covering his chest and shoulders, even his legs, to give me a pretty good idea of the violence and speed of his death. Whoever had gotten to him before me had known exactly what he was doing. The knife had been used as deftly as a surgeon's scalpel. Slash, slash and Poy Chu's carotid artery and jugular vein were cut right in two. He must have lost several pints of blood within a matter of minutes, perhaps in even less time than that.

One thing was certain: Poy Chu wasn't in any shape to talk.

All he wore was a towel, identical to mine. I didn't

want to take any chances, so I untied it from around his waist, but he wasn't concealing anything but some more bloodstained skin. Then I spotted his locker key, secured by elastic around the crook of his arm. Even with the heat rising steadily, his skin was still turning cold. His flesh was clammy and fish-belly white where it wasn't red and sticky with blood. But squeamishness isn't in my emotional repertoire. There was nothing I could do for the poor fool, so I didn't think twice about straightening out his stiffening arm and sliding the key down below his elbow and over his wrist and fingers.

Before I climbed down from the benches, I turned his head back toward the wall, hoping he'd remain unnoticed by the management of the Hungry Ghosts Turkish Bath. If things worked out, he wouldn't be found for several hours—not until some unlucky customer came across the grisly corpse. By then, I'd be back at my hotel with no one the wiser for what I'd unhappily discovered on Temple Street.

Poy Chu's locker wasn't very far from my own. The key fit into the lock without any trouble at all. I swung the metal door back and found myself staring at a pile of clothes, most of them slashed just as deftly as the double-agent's throat. The assassin wasn't playing a sloppy game. He'd taken the time to go through Poy Chu's belongings, cutting through the lining of the man's sport jacket and the pockets of his doubleknit trousers. Obviously, he was looking for the same thing I'd come to Hong Kong to buy. But Poy Chu had told me he'd put his information away for safekeeping until such time as he got paid for his troubles. As a result, I doubted that he'd stashed what I—and obviously someone else—was looking for among the contents of a locker.

With Poy Chu dead, I was really up the proverbial creek without a paddle. The information he had to sell was too valuable, too important for U.S. security, to just be forgotten about and filed away under dead letters and dead double-agents. My only hope was that he'd left some kind of clue behind—however slim, however meager—to indicate where he'd concealed what I was after. So I examined what was left of his clothes as carefully and exhaustively as was humanly possible. I even pried off the heels of his shoes. For all I knew, they might be hollow and if not a repository for the actual information he had to sell, perhaps they served as a hiding place for something to indicate its location, something to lead me to it. Anything.

But the shoes were as ordinary as they come, bereft of an espionage agent's bag of tricks. I was tossing everything back inside the locker, knowing that there was nothing else I could do, when I saw a scrap of paper out of the corner of my eye. Apparently, it had fallen out of Poy Chu's slacks, when his murderer—or I—had ransacked the contents of the locker. The paper was half-hidden against the floor of the locker and the adjacent metal wall. I pulled it free and brought it out into the light.

The locker room was still empty as I read *Fung Ping Shan Mus*. The rest of the admissions ticket was probably back at the museum of Hong Kong University. All that was left was half of it, just a ragged-edged stub. I turned it over and smiled to myself. Scribbled across the blank side of the stiff paper ticket were two Chinese ideograms—pencilled characters which spelled out the name *Tou Wan*. It didn't ring any bells, but it was better than nothing.

I closed the locker, locked it and slipped the key through the grating in the rusty door. It rang loudly in my ears as it hit the metal floor of the narrow closet. There was nothing else to be done on Temple Street. I turned away and felt something uncomfortably familiar flush against the small of my back.

"What an intriguing little place this is, wouldn't you agree?" announced a voice with a British accent.

"Delightful," I said, feeling the icy-cold barrel of an

automatic pressed up against my spine. "Judging from the shape of your gun barrel, I'd say you were about to shoot me with a Model 39 Smith & Wesson. And I'd also venture the guess that you're not alone, either."

My new found acquaintance chuckled slyly under his breath. "How very cunning of you to tell," he said, while a second and as yet unseen party laughed just as sarcastically.

"When you're number two, you always have to try a little harder," I replied and shrugged my shoulders.

Neither of them were laughing then, not any longer. "Perhaps then, you'll try equally as hard to be cooperative," and saying this, the man who spoke the King's English pushed me forward, the automatic still digging into my back.

One move, false or otherwise, and I didn't doubt the speed with which he would squeeze the trigger. Hong Kong, and Temple Street in particular, was proving itself to be not only colorful, but dangerous as well.

CHAPTER TWO

I still had the ticket stub between my thumb and forefinger. But I wouldn't have it for long, for as I was hustled out of the locker room I managed to drop the scrap of paper onto the tile floor. My captors didn't seem to notice, which was fine with me. I was going to have my hands full, literally as well as figuratively, and the less they knew about my business—the mission Hawk had outlined less than a week before—the better.

British accent still kept the Smith & Wesson jammed against my back. A squeeze of his finger, just the slightest amount of pressure, and I could easily imagine the round bloody hole he'd drill clear through my spine. "I hope you haven't worked yourself up into a sweat," he said with another in what was fast becoming an ongoing series of sly little laughs.

"Not yet," I said. "And today I seem to have developed a definite aversion to steam rooms."

"Our friend is a comic," British accent told his accomplice. "But I don't think he'll be laughing very much longer, do you?"

It was a rhetorical question, one which his partner didn't have to bother answering. I still couldn't see either of them, but the instant I tried to turn my head to the side, the owner of the Model 39 slammed his hand across my face. I felt the faceted stone on his pinkie ring dig brutally into my chest. It was not the most pleasant way to come in contact with a ruby.

17

"No one gave you permission to do anything, little man," he said. The steam heat was fast melting his sarcasm. In its place I now detected a raw edge of cruelty, a sadistic side to his temperament which only made me that much more alert, wary.

A stubby-fingered hand, ringless and hairy, now shot out across my field of vision. British accent's sidekick did the honors, pulling open a door which bore a deceptively innocent notice. The word SAUNA was hand-lettered on a small square of wood. I didn't have a chance to make a move, one way or the other. I was immediately thrown forward, the heavy and virtually impregnable door closing behind us.

It was only then that I had a chance to view my interrogators face-to-face. British accent still kept his automatic leveled on my chest. The very personification of colonialism, he wore a spotless white linen suit with an old school tie, and planted his legs wide apart as he gave me a grim and determined stare. No doubt he was hoping his unblinking look would reinforce his position of authority. Not about to disappoint, I let my features gradually relax and crumble, trying to appear as terrified as he was ruthless. But while I studied his lean, angular face and his glacier-cold gray eyes, I knew I had never seen him before.

As for his co-worker, he too was a complete and total stranger. He had the look of a bodyguard, an ex-prize fighter, right down to his cauliflower ears and mashed-in nose. Shorter than his partner by a good five or six inches, he was built like a fireplug, squat and burly. He wasn't going to be a pushover or fun to tangle with, that was certain.

"Relax, my friend," old school tie announced, breaking his self-imposed silence. He curled his lips back, exposing a single glittering gold cap in a row of even teeth. It was not the kind of dental work I expected from someone who looked as though he would have been very comfortable on a cricket field. "Take a seat."

I edged back until my hands made contact with the slippery surface of a wooden bench. I sank down, totally cooperative until such time as I felt confident I wouldn't have to worry about the business end of his Smith & Wesson. The sauna's dry heat made the sweat pour out of me. I kept wiping my hands dry on my towel, knowing that when the time came I'd need all the gripping power I possessed. For the moment, I let the two men call all the shots, as curious about them as I was certain they were about me.

"So," British accent said with a grin, "tell us what brings you to the Yue Lan, Mr. . . ?"

"Morley—Joshua T. Morley," I said, keeping my arms close to my sides. If they caught sight of the tiny AXE tattoo on my inner right elbow, whatever cover I was still in possession of would be blown to smithereens, along with the rest of me, no doubt.

"Very well, Mr. *Morley*," he said, grinning even more smugly. "I take it you're not a regular customer. And I take it that you missed your appointment with Poy Chu."

"Poy who?"

"I will make the jokes, Mr. Morley. You, in turn, will provide me with the answers. Is that clear?"

"Whatever you say, old chap."

"Fine," he said, ignoring my gibe. "As long as you understand the ground rules, I don't think we should have any problems communicating." He turned his head to the side and whispered in his accomplice's battered ear.

I couldn't make out what he said, but no sooner did he turn back to me when his friend stepped forward, apparently quite pleased with the instructions he'd just been given. In no time at all, fireplug stationed himself directly behind me. "Now?" he asked, the single questioning word cloaked in an accent that was clearly Eastern European. It went along with his rumpled forties gangster suit, his

scuffed steeltoed bluchers, his ragged-edged collar and
skinny black tie. But what he lacked in sartorial splendor,
he clearly made up in pure brute strength.

"Whenever you're ready, my good man," white linen
suit replied, growing more snide and more self-confident
with each passing second.

That too was fine with me. I wanted both men to think
I was too scared to function, at a loss for words as well as
moves. But when the pride of Eastern Europe wrenched
my arm back with a bone-breaking jerk, it was all I could
do not to cry out in pain. I gritted my teeth, all eyes on the
automatic which was still aimed precisely at the center of
my chest.

"Now isn't that better?" the talkative half of the duo
went on. "I'm sure you must agree, Mr. Morley, that my
friend behind you knows exactly what he's doing. Now,
where were we?"

"In Hong Kong," I said, swearing under my breath.

"Indeed," he said and threw his head back and laughed
with exaggerated—and wooden-nickel phony—good-hu-
mor. "The Crown Colony someone far cleverer than I
once referred to as China in a gray flannel suit. But tell
me about your connection with the late Poy Chu, Mr.
Morley. I find that infinitely more intriguing."

"I don't know who you're talking about."

"Very well," he muttered and motioned to his assistant—a mere shrug of his immaculate, linen-clad shoulders.

My arm was pulled up and back, the move so swift and
vicious, so effortless as well, that I thought my shoulder
would be instantly dislocated. Pain exploded like a burning wound, up and down my side. But if I tried anything,
I'd be a sitting duck for the Smith & Wesson. I had no
desire to feel the impact of a high-powered slug, either
now or later, and certainly not at a distance of less than
three yards.

"Who do you work for, Morley?"

"A Chinese take-out place, right next door."

Again my arm was pulled back, the shoulder joint cracking as loudly as ten pairs of knuckles.

"Free-lance," I groaned.

Eastern Europe missed the essence of the idiom. But when British accent nodded his head, he finally relaxed his grip on my arm. "That's better," said my white-suited inquisitor. "And what did Poy Chu have that you found so valuable?"

"I . . . I . . ." My eyes bugged out with pain as my arm was once again pulled back.

"Talk, Mr. Morley. Unless of course you wish to lose the use of your arm. And then your leg . . . and then your other arm, ad infinitum."

"He . . . he wanted to sell me a shipment—"

"Ah, now we're getting to the heart of the matter," British accent said and gave me his best music-hall smirk. "A shipment of what, Mr. Morley?"

"Industrial diamonds," I blurted out.

His mood underwent an immediate and drastic change. "You're a fool, Morley," he replied, spitting the words out, each one more precise than the next. "What's worse, you take me for an even bigger one. And that is something I find most intolerable, particularly in a rank amateur such as yourself." He stepped forward, his finger caressing the hair trigger of his revolver. "Both arms now," he told his accomplice.

Without even bothering to get me into a full nelson, Eastern Europe wrenched my other arm back, pulling it to the breaking point. His fingers were like steel cuffs and though I knew I could get out of the hold, it was still the wrong time to put on a show of karate skills, a pyrotechnical display of *tae kwon do,* the Korean form of the martial arts.

"Now walk, Morley, just like a duck," white suit snickered, patently amused.

His partner shoved me off the bench. With my arms

pinned back behind me, it was impossible to straighten up. I was forced to waddle on bent legs, moving closer and closer to the business end of the Smith & Wesson. White suit seemed to take great pleasure in my discomfort. He flashed a broad sarcastic grin and nodded his head with delight.

"The position suits you, Morley," he said, chuckling to himself. And to his friend it was, "Take him right over there," pointing to the far end of the overheated cubicle.

What amazed me as much as anything else was that the man behind the revolver wasn't sweating in the least. Here I was, soaking wet, both arms pinned behind my back, and he was just standing there in his wrinkle-free suit, not a single bead of perspiration dotting his forehead.

He's cold-blooded in more ways than one, I thought. A moment later my eyes opened wide, when I suddenly was able to figure out where they were leading me.

I was being shoved directly toward the electric heating grid which controlled the temperature of the sauna.

The mechanism looked like the inside of a toaster, a series of convoluted tungsten coils, already glowing a firery red. The grid was encased in steel supports and these too seemed to be just as hot as the rest of the heating element.

"Hong Kong is most up-to-date," white suit remarked, reading my grim expression. "No hot stones and boiling water for them, the way the Finns prefer. Oh no, the Crown Colony must boast the newest and the best, the latest and the most efficient. Care to continue the experiment, Morley? Or have you decided to cooperate like a good little boy?"

"I told you," I said, choking back a cry of rage. "He wanted to sell me a shipment of diamonds, industrial diamonds. He'd stolen them from—"

British accent shook his head, his expression petulant now, playing the aggrieved schoolmaster to my truculent and stubborn schoolboy. "That won't do, Morley," he said, shaking his head once again. "No, no, that won't do at all." He clucked his tongue and waved the automatic before me, the gesture as threatening as the red-hot tungsten coils. Sweat dripped down, stinging my eyes. I was perhaps a foot away from the electric grid, but already I could feel the fierce heat it was giving off. "A little closer," he said to his burly henchman who was keeping my arms pinned back like a butterfly trapped against an insect mount.

Six inches away now, the reddish glow of the heating element began to singe my brows and eyelashes. The cloying odor of burning hair rose up before me. Every muscle of my body stood out in sharp relief. I was straining, trying to keep as far away from the coils as I possibly could.

"Would you like to wear the mark of Cain, for all time, Mr. Morley?" I was asked. "Perhaps that's the only way to get you to be more open, more free with your answers. So do yourself a favor and tell me about Poy Chu. Unless of course you prefer to be branded. A little closer, my friend. Just a tad, as I've heard it said in the good old U.S. of A."

Eastern Europe once again did the questionable honors, shoving me so close that it was all I could do not to scream out in pain. I could feel my forehead blistering and despite the close proximity of the Smith & Wesson, I couldn't remain passive any longer. At that instant the sauna door creaked open, no doubt another customer anxious to use the facility—but the way it was intended.

It was the diversion I had waited for, the one I desperately needed. Even as white suit jerked his head around and locked the door securely from the inside, I counted *il, e, sam,* one-two-three, and let loose the way my karate instructor, Master Chun, had so painstakingly taught me.

Time was literally of the essence. There was no thought to assume the correct form, the proper stance. I reacted instinctively, snapping my right leg back until I heard the satisfying crunch of my opponent's knee. His patella didn't shatter, unfortunately. But with his roar of pain came a loosening of his hands. White suit was apparently reluctant to bring the revolver into play, lest he wound his partner and then have to face me single-handed.

That too was fine with me.

The instant Eastern Europe let his grip slide, I was whirling around, slamming my elbows back to finally break his vicious hold. He gave a bellow of rage and threw himself forward, only to find his chin connecting with my wrist. The blow sent him reeling backwards, giving me the leeway and distance I needed to lash out with a high kick to his forehead.

It was a helluva lot more complicated than *se-bon kyo-lu-ki,* the three-step sparring form I'd practiced over and over again with Master Chun. But this was not sport karate, either. Even as the iron curtain's answer to Al Capone toppled backwards like an overstuffed sack of potatoes, I was darting to the side to avoid the butt of British accent's deadly revolver. Apparently, the information I had at my fingertips was too valuable. He still seemed unwilling to put the automatic to use and his indecision now proved to be his undoing.

"Bloody treacherous pig!" I heard him cry out, his one free hand clawing at the lock of the door.

I wasn't about to let him get off so easily, not after all the pain he'd put me through.

My right foot was already moving seconds before I fully realized what I was doing. The flying kick saw my instep meet British accent's temple in a single bone-jarring thud. He gave a shrill agonized scream, one composed of both pain and surprise. Then he dropped to the sauna floor. The Smith & Wesson flew through the air, clattering loudly as it hit the wooden boards. At that split-second Eastern Europe threw himself around my neck, pressing his thumbs into my windpipe.

I was totally prepared.

A *sohn-nal chi-ki* or knife-hand attack was immediately followed by an elbow thrust to his ribs. But the sonuvabitch wasn't about to give up so easily. I could feel his hot, fetid breath on my neck as I gripped both of his little fingers. His thumbs dug in, squeezing at my throat, about to crush my windpipe to the consistency of a chocolate mousse. But before that could happen, I pulled his pinkies sharply out and back. It was snap, crackle, and pop as one bone broke neatly after the other.

The two little fingers hung down, no longer in workman-like condition. But the guy still wouldn't listen to reason. He had an amazingly high pain-threshold and now a stream of incoherent words rushed out of his throat as he throttled me, shoving me back and forth as if he were trying to shake the stuffing out of me. But I wasn't Raggedy Andy and I didn't intend to become a child's battered plaything.

Wrenching to the side, even as both thumbs continued to exhaust the meager air supply left in my lungs, I lashed out with a *yiop cha-ki*, a side kick to the back of his knee. His leg started to crumple up beneath him and his grip on my throat loosened accordingly. A second kick followed in the wake of the first, this one to the back of his other knee. Unsteady now, barely able to remain on his feet, he finally let go and reached inside his jacket, his two little fingers hanging down like a pair of dead and stubby pink worms.

Not about to stand there and wait for him to produce either a calling card or, more likely, a snub-nosed revolver, I drove my right arm out sharply to the side. All of my weight and strength was concentrated on my tightly clenched fist. An inverted-fist strike was the direct result, one which saw the collision of my unbending arm with Eastern Europe's spleen.

I couldn't tell if I'd ruptured it or not, but I sure as hell wasn't about to hang around to find out. He fell back, hit the side of his head against the edge of one of the wooden benches and went out like a cartoon character around whose head kiddies enjoy the sight of chirping birds, twinkling stars, and other animated tomfoolery. Only difference, Eastern Europe—or wherever the hell he came from—hadn't been created by Walt Disney.

Behind me, white suit was now crumpled gray suit. He'd even decided to start sweating, which struck me as a welcome change, a return to normalcy. I found him crawling on all fours, trying to reach his fallen revolver. The skin had split along his temple, sending a thin gluey stream of blood trickling down his neck and under his shirt collar.

"From Joshua T. Morley, with love," I said, my bare feet coming down on his fingers in a single synchronized crunch of tendon, bone, and sinew. His scream was raw, tearing around the edges of his puffy, foam-flecked lips. I retrieved the Smith & Wesson, reached under my towel and removed Pierre. The tiny gas bomb had been waiting to be put to use—impatiently, no doubt—all this time and I wasn't about to disappoint either the product of AXE's technological ingenuity, or my two fallen captors.

"It's been a real gas," I said, releasing the charge on Pierre. I tossed the bomb onto the floor of the sauna, heard its comforting hiss and then saw it explode in a cloud of burning chemical Mace. The sauna door swung shut behind me, even as British accent cried out in terror.

Temple Street, the Hungry Ghosts Turkish Bath, was not what I would call my most favorite place.

CHAPTER THREE

A week before, steam heat was the last thing on my mind.

"Take a seat, Nick. I'll be with you in a minute," Hawk said as I stepped inside his office, back at AXE's Washington headquarters.

I slid down into a leather wing chair and waited for him to finish what he was doing. Through the slats in the Venetian blind, directly behind his battered oak desk, I caught glimpses of traffic, backed up around Dupont Circle. March had just ended a few days before. Good to its name, it had gone out like a lamb, the mercury rolling up an impressive and springlike sixty-seven. But April too was aware of the nursery rhyme and for the last three days the sky had emptied itself of rain in a seemingly endless deluge.

The dampness affected me adversely, and this spell of humid weather made me my old wounds throb uncomfortably, an unhappy reminder of the stiletto I'd taken in New Delhi, the bullet which had pierced my calf back in Katmandu, less than a year before. But now my thoughts weren't on past assignments, missions which had ultimately been successful. Instead, I was aware of Hawk's craggy, downturned face revealing a look of intense concentration. His hooded eyes glanced up for an instant, his expression colored now by something akin to preoccupation, perhaps even uncertainty.

"Your passport in order?" he said, trying to make a

joke. He transferred the wet, reeking stub of his cigar from one corner of his mouth to the other.

"It always is."

"Good, because you'll be needing it. With a new name, of course."

"Where to this time, sir?"

"Hong Kong," he replied, letting it sink in. "President's orders."

"Aren't they always?"

"Only when it's too dirty ... or difficult ... for the boys over at Central Intelligence. Besides, the Oval Office hasn't been too happy, what with this spate of security leaks. Take that submarine caper, for example. It was downright embarrassing for the Administration. We're just lucky we didn't get some of the backlash."

I just sat there and nodded my head, knowing there was a reason why he was taking the long way around the issue, why he was taking his time getting to the crux of the matter. He tamped out the end of the cigar, reached for his humidor, and brought out another.

"Thing is, Nick, we just can't afford any screw-ups." He paused for a moment and then lit a match. The flame flared up; the tobacco began to glow. He put both hands on the desk, though the gesture had nothing to do with honesty. It was just a kind of reference point, an indication of his seriousness, mirroring the earnest expression which had come into his eyes. "Two days ago, one of your counterparts was murdered—"

"Who?" I interrupted.

"Rawlings."

"Sonuvabitch," I swore, shaking my head. "I thought he was too smart for that."

"So did I," Hawk replied. "It was meant to look like suicide. Needless to say, it wasn't. They found him in his hotel room. An overdose. He'd been dead several hours."

"Where?"

"Hong Kong."

"Which is where I come in, right?"

"Precisely." He edged back in his chair and blew a weary smoke ring up to the ceiling. It hit the acoustical tiling and bounced back, momentarily clouding his face. "Rawlings, of course, was on assignment. I'd sent him over to purchase a roll of microfilm. Unfortunately, he never even got a chance to meet his contact."

"I take it the contact's still waiting."

Hawk nodded his head. "Does the name Poy Chu ring a bell?"

"Several." I leaned forward, aware of the way AXE's Director and Operations Chief was fixing me with his unblinking stare. "A Chinese double-agent, thirty-four, no visible scars, average height, unassuming appearance, reputed to be only sporadically reliable, though the goods he delivers are always of the highest quality."

"Excellent," he murmured. "Now, try this on for size, Nick." he said, stopping just long enough to flick the ash off the end of his foul-smelling cigar. "What would you say if I told you Poy Chu has managed to get ahold of a roll of microfilm, one which lists *every*—not just two or three or even half a dozen, Nick, but every goddamn one—every single Chinese espionage agent working in the West. *And* the Soviet Union."

"I'd say he was the man of the hour," I said, whistling softly under my breath.

"You're damn right he is," Hawk agreed. He pounded his fist emphatically against his desk. "Do you know what this could mean for us, what a breakthrough it would be? Imagine having the goods on *everyone*, the names of every number they have working in this country, in Europe, too. And the whole thing would never have been put together if it hadn't been for our detente with Russia. A lot of top Chinese are worried. Apparently, he's been fearing a power struggle, which is why he had the list assembled in the first place. He wanted all those names at his fingertips,

just in case someone tried to turn the tables on him ...
and I don't mean the Red Guard, either."

"It would mean the complete downfall, the collapse of
their intelligence plans, particularly here in the States."

"Their network of agents would never recover," Hawk
concurred. "What's more, Nick, we've been waiting for a
break like this ever since '49. That's why the Oval Office
doesn't want any screw-ups. The President, the National
Security Council, the Pentagon too, want that roll of film,
and they're willing to pay the price."

"Which is?"

"Cheap, at least by our standards."

"How cheap?"

"Very. Two hundred thousand in American green. He
won't even hassle us about Swiss francs. Seems he's anxious to retire and as far as he's concerned, two hundred
thou is a pretty decent nest egg," Hawk explained.
"There's only one catch."

"I figured as much."

"We have no idea if he's duplicated the list or if he's
been calling in bids—"

"*Exempli gratia*—the Soviet Union and the KGB?"

Hawk nodded his head, put down his cigar and examined the tips of his nicotine-stained fingers. "The one
thing I can vouch for is that Poy Chu is greedy. And if
our Soviet counterparts come up with a sum in excess of
two hundred thousand, Poy Chu won't bat an eyelash.
He'll turn around and sell them the film so fast it'll make
you dizzy."

"Providing of course Peking doesn't get to him before
they do."

"Before *you* do, Nick," he corrected. "Because we just
can't accept failure. It's as simple as that. Apparently,
Poy Chu's already afraid there's been a leak, that someone in Peking intelligence is on to him, aware of the fact
that the spy list has been microfilmed and smuggled

across the border into Hong Kong. So he's playing a very cautious game."

"Needless to say, I'll have to do the same." I got slowly to my feet. "When would you like me to leave, sir?"

"Tonight. You're already booked out of Dulles. We've made reservations for you at the Peninsula."

"Best hotel in the colony," I murmured.

"Nothing's too good for N3," he said, trying to laugh. It didn't come off.

"Under what name will I be traveling, sir?"

"Morley." He got to his feet and extended his hand. It was unlike him, the gesture both formal and funereal. I could tell he was already starting to work himself up into a sweat about the mission, as if he feared he might be sending me to the same unhappy fate Rawlings had suffered just two days before. "Joshua T. Morley."

We shook on it.

Six hours later I was strapped inside a 747, already climbing to upwards of 32,000 feet. From where I sat, there was no way I could see Dupont Circle, or David Hawk's troubled and scowling face.

One fact stood out above all else.

Poy Chu hadn't been nearly as cautious as he'd intended.

Someone had been one up on him. Someone had gotten to the Red Chinese double-agent, intent upon preventing him from disclosing the location of the roll of microfilm. Who that person was, that unknown third party, was as much a mystery as the whereabouts of the priceless list of espionage agents.

As for the two men I had tangled with at the Turkish bath, white suit and his all-but-mute companion, I had a strong suspicion that they were my equivalent numbers the KGB, the Committee of State Security which is to the Soviet Union what the CIA is to the United States. Per-

haps British accent was a defector like Maclean or
Burgess, Russian spies who had infiltrated the British
Foreign Office back in the early fifties. But whether or not
Poy Chu had arranged to meet them was still something
I could only assume until such time as the facts were sub-
stantiated and my theories—and I had many, even at this
early date—verified with cold, hard evidence, clear-cut
and absolute.

No way was I going to believe that they had been responsible for the double-agent's untidy and rather grisly
demise. By murdering Poy Chu they would only have
been defeating their own purposes, since the microfilm
was just as invaluable to the KGB as it was to AXE. So I
was pretty sure they'd come upon a dead body, just as I
had. And now, they were probably just as much in the
dark as yours truly, Killmaster N3.

Since Poy Chu had told me he'd put the film away for
safekeeping, until such time as the deal was finalized and
our delicate negotiations concluded, I had no choice but
to presume that he hadn't been lying and that he hadn't
gone back on his word. And if he hadn't carried the microfilmed documents on his person, as I'd originally
feared, then chances were they still were where he'd hidden them.

But where the hell is that? I thought to myself as I
ducked out of the Hungry Ghosts Turkish Bath.

My fairy godmother was out-of-town, and even if she
weren't, she probably wouldn't be able to provide me with
the necessary answer, anyway. So I was on my own again,
hustling my tail away from Temple Street, taking the
shortest possible route to the Star Ferry, down by Salis-
bury and Nathan Roads, less than a block from my hotel.

At least I'd found the ticket stub, a piece of evidence
which Poy Chu's assassin had apparently overlooked and
which British accent and Eastern Europe had done as
well. And the more I thought about it, the more significant it seemed to become. For one, there were very few

museums in Hong Kong, to begin with. Lots of restaurants, lots of massage parlors and department stores, but very little in the way of hard-core cultural attractions. For another, it just didn't strike me as either a likely or credible leisure-time activity for a man of Poy Chu's ilk. Double-agents just have too much on their minds to think in terms of *objets d'art* (unless they're stealing them) and old masters.

So once again I was back in that hazy and inconclusive realm of assumption and hypothesis.

Assumption one said that Poy Chu had been murdered by an agent from Peking, someone who was determined to recover the roll of microfilm before it could be sold and delivered to the hands of "unfriendly" powers, e.g., the U.S. or the U.S.S.R.

Assumption two was that Poy Chu hadn't shown himself to be very cooperative, losing his already tenuous and slender hold on life as a direct result of his unwillingness to part with his information.

Assumption three rested on the validity of one and two: the microfilmed documents were still where Poy Chu had secreted them, as opposed to being on their way back to Peking.

And until such time as one or all of the above were proven otherwise, I had no choice but to continue my mission and hope that it would end on a note of success, not failure.

So you see, at this point everything sort of rested on the importance of the ticket stub, a ragged-edged scrap of paper which was now leading me directly to the Fung Ping Shan Museum of Hong Kong University.

Exactly twenty-five minutes after I had left white linen suit and his finger-popping friend, I found myself across the harbor, on the Hong Kong Island side of the Crown Colony. From here it was but a short walk to the Mandarin Hotel, where I boarded the #3 bus to Bonham Road and the museum.

At least I had a jump on my two rivals, though it had cost me first-degree burns clear across my forehead. But that, however, was the least of my worries. Now that Wilhelmina was back where she belonged, snug inside my shoulder holster; and now that my pencil-thin stiletto, Hugo, was strapped to the inside of my arm, I no longer felt half as vulnerable or naked as I had back at the baths.

Too impatient to sit back and enjoy the local color and the constantly changing scenery, I leaned forward in my seat, my shoulders hunched, my brow knit. My thoughts kept turning again and again on the two Chinese ideograms pencilled across the back of the ticket stub.

Tou Wan.

It was a woman's name, oddly enough. Poy Chu's sister? Mother? Lover, mistress, wife? I didn't have the slightest idea, but hopefully someone at the museum would.

It proved to be an unprepossessing building, considerably off the beaten track, not what one would call a popular tourist attraction by any stretch of the imagination. Like most of the architecture on the Hong Kong side, the Fung Ping Shan Museum was just another bland testimony to British colonialism, neither an eyesore nor a monument to artistic or native ingenuity.

A quick survey of its three stories revealed absolutely nothing of interest, nothing to spark my curiosity. Unimaginative displays of Chinese pottery, porcelain, and bronze filled the glass museum cases. If anything, the collection was mediocre and ordinary at best. At worst, it was downright embarrassing. Of course, I couldn't exclude the possibility that Poy Chu had selected precisely this kind of out-of-the-way place in which to hide the film he'd managed to smuggle out of Peking.

Again, I pondered the meaning of the name Tou Wan, certain it held an answer, one which kept eluding my grasp. One of the museum attendants found me hunched over a case, both elbows flush against the glass. My eyes were half-closed, my thoughts far removed from the display of antique ceramics laid out before me.

A tap on the shoulder brought me back to reality. I straightened up and turned slowly around. A bespectacled young man smiled politely, his English crisp and precise. "Please not to lean on case, sir," he said, almost apologetically. "Very old, rickety. Understand?"

"Sorry," I murmured. Before he could turn away I told him how fascinating I found the exhibits.

"You like?" he asked, quite pleased with my positive appraisal of the museum's collection.

"Very much so," I went on, anxious to get on his good side. "It's the first time I've been here, though I often come to Hong Kong on business, several times a year."

"How unfortunate," he replied, his comment sounding like a *non sequitur* until I asked him to explain. "Very unhappy for you to have missed special exhibit."

My eyes opened wide with interest. "I hadn't heard about it," I said.

"It was most edifying, most instructive," the young man told me. "But . . . unfortunately the display ended two days ago. Yes, the day before yesterday."

"What kind of exhibit was it, actually?"

"Very priceless treasures," he said, evidently taking great stock in their monetary worth. "On loan from People's Republic of China, from wonderful Museum of Chinese History in Peking."

"I'm sorry I missed it," I said, still playing up to him. "I suppose it's already on its way back to China."

The man shook his head, his eyeglasses slipping down along the bridge of his nose. He pushed them back into place with a self-conscious gesture and said, "Not China, but Union of Burma. You know Burma?"

I didn't but I said I did. "Rangoon," I replied, figuring that would be the safest answer to his question.

"Ah, that is very nice," he said and smiled and nodded

his head. "To travel to many places, that is great wish of mine. Someday I will like to do the same. But exhibit is now on way to Rangoon, part of cultural exchange program. Most wonderful treasures of great artistic and historical interest."

I clucked my tongue to reinforce my look of disappointment. "If only I'd known," I said. "But perhaps you might be able to help me. I'm interested in finding out about a woman by the name of Tou Wan. Do you know who she is, where I could get in touch with her?"

"Tou Wan?" be repeated, scratching vigorously at his straight black hair as if the answer lurked right below his scalp. "I do not know her personally," he said, whereupon he began to laugh softly to himself.

I couldn't understand what he found so amusing. "Do you know anyone who does?" I asked.

The museum attendant cocked his head to one side and studied me for a silent moment. Then his lips curled up into a grin. "You are serious? You not playing joke with me?"

"No," I said, growing increasingly dumbfounded by his reaction to my question. "I'm absolutely serious. What makes you think I'm joking?"

"Because Tou Wan is dead," he replied.

"Dead? When did she die?"

"More than two thousand years ago, sir," he said, his laughter echoing loudly in my ears.

CHAPTER FOUR

Obviously, Tou Wan wasn't in any shape to tell me what she knew.

A moment later the museum attendant's laughter ended abruptly, as though he feared I would think him impolite. "I do not wish to offend," he said. "But your question . . . it was most funny. You see, Tou Wan was princess of Han Dynasty. At her death, over two thousand years ago, body of Tou Wan was placed in armor suit . . . yes, I believe that is right word. It was made of jade. You know of jade, yes?"

I nodded my head.

"Jade was believed to keep human body in perfect condition—for all time. Not so, but that is belief of Tou Wan and her royal family. So when you ask after her, I must laugh, because she is not even dust. Understand?"

"In other words, this jade . . . funerary suit—"

"Suit for death, after dying, yes," he said, nodding his head vigorously up and down.

"—this jade death suit was part of the exhibit from Peking, is that it?"

Again his head bobbed up and down, even more energetically than before. "Most valuable treasure in all of collection," he told me. "Many many fine pieces jade linked with wire of purest gold. It is said it took ten years to make. But of course I do not know for certain of that, because it was very long time ago, many, many years."

37

"Well, I'm sorry I missed it," I said. "But you've been very helpful. I appreciate it."

"It is great pleasure for me," he said. "Few people take enjoyment in museum. So when I can be of service, it is very good thing."

It most certainly is, I thought. Absolutely.

Even as I left the museum and hailed a taxi to take me back in the direction of the Star Ferry, right off Connaught Road Central, I knew that I had my work set out for me. Hawk would not be satisfied until he had the roll of microfilm in his hands. It was my job to see that he got it. Even if I ended up following a trail of exotic red herrings, I really had no other choice. Tou Wan' jade funerary suit was the only solid clue—the *single* clue—I had to go on. Perhaps it was a long shot, longer than most I'd taken, but I realized that I wouldn't be happy until I had inspected the jade treasure with my own two hands.

Then and only then would I know if I'd followed a dead end. But not before.

I'd have to work fast of course, because I had a feeling the two KGB agents wouldn't be very far behind. First item on the agenda was securing an entry visa at the Burmese Consulate. The driver of the taxi knew exactly where to let me off, directly in front of the International Building on Des Voeux Road Central, around the corner from the ferry.

My timing couldn't have been better, because the consulate was just about to close its doors when I slipped inside and hurriedly filled out the necessary forms. "Forty-eight hours," the woman stationed behind the information desk announced. "It is hard and fast rule, no exceptions possible."

"Can't I pay an extra fee to get in, in say . . . twenty-four hours?" I asked, laying on the charm as thick as I dared.

She was a bureaucrat, an automaton. Nothing I could

have said or done would have moved her, one iota. "The government, the Union of Burma, makes the rules," she said briskly, examining the blue-gray cover of my passport as if she were looking for gravy stains. "And I must remind you that your entry visa only allows you to stay in Burma for one week, not in excess of seven days."

"I can't stay longer?"

"What is the purpose of your visit, sir?" she asked, her tone of voice, her very attitude, unduly suspicious.

"It says right there," I said, pointing to the appropriate line on the application form, and reading, "Tourism." I flashed her my all-purpose knock-'em-dead grin.

That too failed to press her.

"Seven days should be ample time to see the country. Budget your time." She clipped my passport to the application and returned to her paperwork.

"Thank you. You've been most kind." I was out the door before she could figure out if I'd been sarcastic or not. Thing is, I could've gotten the boys at the American Consulate on Garden Road to cut through some of the sticky red tape. But that kind of diplomatic razzle-dazzle would only have attracted unnecessary attention. I wanted to enter Burma like the most ordinary tourist imaginable, even if it meant wearing bermuda shorts and carrying a Kodak Instamatic. So if it was going to take two days to get my visa, well, I'd just have to put up with the delay.

What bothered me more was the seven-day restriction. I'd never been to Burma before, though I was fairly well acquainted with the political and cultural tenor of the country. I even spoke a smattering of Burmese, though English was widely used, particularly in Rangoon. One week wasn't going to be very much time at all. I still had to figure out a way to examine the jade death suit, still had to find out where it was going to be displayed in Rangoon. And on top of everything else, I now had an Assumption four to add to my fast-growing list.

Had Poy Chu hidden the roll of film somewhere on the

funerary suit, either within the armor or as part of its case? That was the question of the hour and I'd just have to sit tight until I could find out, one way or the other.

By the time I paid my fare and boarded the ferry to return to Kowloon, dusk was already descending. The harbor looked like a scooped-out bowl, its high rounded sides ablaze with hundreds upon hundreds of lights, reaching right up to the top of Victoria Peak. The airline offices were already closed, as was the public library, back on the Hong Kong side in the City Hall High Block.

Well, tomorrow is another day, I thought, just the way the movie always promised.

The following morning I went to work with a vengeance.

I booked passage out of Hong Kong, able to make reservations at Rangoon's Strand Hotel at the same time. With my travel plans in order, my passport still being held at the Burmese Consulate, there was nothing I could do but wait . . . thirty-one hours, to be exact.

The more I thought about it, the more convincing Assumption four seemed to become. If Poy Chu had managed to hide the microfilm within the jade death suit, prior to its being crated and sent out of China, he wouldn't have had to worry about carrying the documents on his person. The most methodical border check wouldn't have revealed anything incriminating, because the roll of film would have already become an invisible (and indivisible) part of the Han Dynasty exhibit. Perhaps the double-agent had known someone back at the Peking museum, someone with access to the exhibit, willing to be a party to his scheme. After all, money—including Communist Chinese Yuan, RMB's by any other name—talks, no matter what the language. Cash is cash, a universal constant. If anyone knew that, it would certainly have been Poy Chu.

Of course, the whole theory might be filled with hot air. After all, Tou Wan was just a woman's name, even if it happened to belong to a princess dead these last two thousand years. But like I said, with nothing else to go on, I really couldn't be picky. The document in question was perhaps more important, more vital to U.S. security, than, say, a dozen nuclear secrets and a couple of classified military codes thrown in for good measure. To let a piece of information like the spy list just slip through my fingers would be unforgivable. And unless I did everything that was humanly—maybe inhumanly, too—possible to locate it, I knew I wouldn't be satisfied.

Nor would Hawk.

Nor the Oval Office.

Which, when you come right down to it, is why I'd booked passage to Rangoon, why I was so determined to follow even the slenderest thread, the most meager of clues.

The ticket and hotel reservations out of the way, I crossed the harbor to Victoria on the Hong Kong side, feeling like an old pro, having lost track of the number of times I'd used the Star Ferry. The library was the next item on my schedule, four floors of stacks in the City Hall, right across the street from the ferry slip and the Queen's Pier.

As had been the case back at the University Museum, the librarians went out of their way to be helpful. At the same time, I went out of my way to make sure white suit and steel-toed bluchers weren't dogging my tracks.

They weren't, at least for the time being.

I boned up on my Burmese, took a cram course in Rangoon street-smarts, and then went to work on a pile of weighty tomes, each and every one an antiquarian's delight. Tou Wan's jade funerary suit had first been discovered in 1968, when two multi-chambered tombs were excavated near the town of Manch'eng, not far from Peking. In fact, two burial suits were found, the second one belonging to Liu Sheng, Princess Tou Wan's husband and half-brother of the Han Emperor, Wu. Chinese archaeologists and art experts had reconstructed the 2,156 hand-crafted jade plaques, since the suit had not withstood the test of time, as Tou Wan had hoped.

I even located an article in a recent periodical which described the traveling exhibit in considerable detail. Not only was Tou Wan's jade death suit on display, but 385 other artifacts, all of them unearthed since 1949. But it was the suit which interested me most of all. Fortunately, that same article was illustrated with a color photograph of the art treasure. Impressive wasn't the word for it. After having been brought up on a diet of double-featured Saturday matinees, *The Mummy's Curse* plus *The Mummy's Ghost,* or *The Mummy's Hand* with *The Mummy's Tomb,* I couldn't help but feel a sense of déjà vu, recalling all the silver-screen monsters who had peopled my childhood nightmares.

The jade death suit fit into that category, though it was unlike any "mummy" I had ever laid eyes on before. It took as its form the human body, its contours totally recognizable, down to its ears, to the jade plaques which formed its three-sided nose—even to its hands, clenched into twin jade-gloved fists. A gilded bronze headrest served as a pillow for Tou Wan's final sleep. Before each of her hands lay ritual *huangs,* crescent half-moons of jade. At her side were four bluish-green jade disks, two on the right and two on the left. Known as *pi,* they were symbols of heaven. She had been pampered in life, certain of a royal reception in heaven, certain too that the burial suit would preserve her corporeal form, for all time. But when the tomb was first opened, all that remained of her earthly existence was a handful of dust, nothing more and nothing less.

I closed the magazine, returned the books to their appropriate shelves, and left as unobtrusively as possible.

Another day had passed, and all too quickly.

I'd been promised my passport, my entrance visa stamped neatly inside, by late the following afternoon. A phone call to Hawk, apprising him of recent developments, then a hot shower and a lavish Peking duck dinner put me in the most mellow and affirmative of moods. The two KGB agents hadn't shown their faces since they'd been considerably bloodied back on Temple Street. I decided to chance an excursion, if only to keep myself out of the picture so as to avoid meeting up with them again.

It had been several years since I'd last been to Macao. The peninsula, located in the Canton delta, was an Overseas Province of Portugal. For more than four hundred years it had somehow remained basically unchanged, never really embracing the twentieth century. Other than the ruins, gambling was Macao's biggest attraction. And since I had no choice but to wait for the Union of Burma to come through with my visa, I decided to take the hydrofoil to the island.

It takes about an hour or so to make the forty-mile trip across the mouth of the Pearl River, from Hong Kong to the sleepy Portuguese enclave. For once, getting a visa wasn't a hassle. Burma had given me a simple document to indicate they were holding my passport. This, in turn, was stamped by the customs official moments before I paid my fare and boarded the hydrofoil.

The weather couldn't have been better. The sea looked like a sheet of azure glass as I took a seat on the upper deck and waited for the hydrofoil to move out of the harbor. I was still waiting when the empty seat right alongside of me was suddenly filled by as attractive a package as I'd seen in quite some time.

Mid-twenties, honey-blonde hair pulled back in a severe bun, sensible low-heeled shoes, conservative attire, but very very appealing. She kept her hands in her lap, her unpolished nails clipped short, just as businesslike as the rest of her. But for all her way of dressing down her considerable physical charms, there was ultimately little she could do to hide the fact that she was a most beautiful young woman.

I told her so, as politely, succinctly, and subtly as I possibly could.

She turned her head to the side, a whisper of "Thank you," darting shyly from between her unpainted lips. She was obviously trying very hard to come off as Marian the Librarian, but it didn't work. Behind the prim and proper facade, there was an altogether different person straining at the bit, eager to reveal itself.

"First time in Hong Kong?" I asked, reaching inside my blazer pocket for my gold cigarette case.

"Yes."

She shook her head at my offer of a cigarette.

"Thank you, but I don't smoke."

To be expected, I thought. We were finally pulling away from the dock and I leaned back in my seat and crossed my legs. I'd watched the passengers coming aboard and British accent and his beefy crony were nowhere in evidence. Not that I'd expected them, but you never can tell, especially in my business.

"I don't believe I've introduced myself. Joshua T. Morley," and I extended my hand.

There was a moment of indecision before she took my hand in hers. Her fingers were soft, warm, her palm slightly damp. "Katherine Holmes," she said, her cheeks flushing ever so slightly.

"Kate?"

She nodded her head.

"Well, it's nice to meet you, Kate," I said, doing my best to put her at her ease. It wasn't as difficult as melting an iceberg but then again, it wasn't child's play, either. "I take it you're from the States."

"Yes, Wisconsin. This is all so . . . so," her hand waving helplessly before her.

"Different?"

"Even more than that. Exotic. I've never traveled in

the Orient before, even though it's really my field of interest." She turned slightly to the side, making herself more comfortable. The hem of her tweed skirt slid up above her knee and from where I sat, right alongside of her, I had an unimpeded view of her slim and shapely calves.

I studied her for a moment, trying to read behind her blue eyes. Innocent was the only descriptive adjective I could come up with. "You're in Asian studies, is that it?" I asked.

"Not exactly," she admitted. "Archaeology."

"Archaeology—no kidding," I said, my eyes opening wide with surprise. "Shades of Heinrich Schliemann."

I still couldn't get a rise out of her.

Deadpan, she said, "Actually, I'm en route to Pagan, to do field research at the Mon ruins there. It's supposed to be a most amazing place. Have you ever heard of it, Mr. . . ?"

"Josh," I repeated. "And yes I have. Central Burma, isn't it?"

"That's right. Just a tiny little village, but the ruins are perhaps the most extensive in the world. Something like five thousand monuments, temples, that kind of thing. My work'll comprise my doctoral dissertation."

Just as I'd first suspected, she was far removed from your ordinary single girl tourist. Yes, I had a most unusual young woman at my side and I didn't intend to lose her easily. The one thing I didn't tell her was that I was also about to leave for Burma. Certain things are best left unmentioned, discretion being the better part of counter-intelligence.

"Burma," I said, shaking my head in apparent disbelief. "That's pretty far afield. How long are you going to be there?"

"Five weeks," she answered, explaining how the government had granted her a special visa since she was going to be working with Burmese archaeologists. "It took nearly a year to get everything arranged, a grant and per-

mission and all. And now that it's about to happen ...
well, I'm still sort of in a daze, if you know what I mean."

"I do," I said. "Travel does strange things to people."
I was thinking of the scars I wore, toting them around
like baggage, from one corner of the globe to another.
"But I know you're going to have a fantastic time."

"I hope so." She lapsed into silence, staring straight
ahead.

It was becoming increasingly apparent that this wasn't
going to be one of my quickie seductions, not by any
stretch of the imagination. But far be it from me to give
up in the face of adversity. Her shyness was a challenge
and the more I looked at her, the more determined I be-
came to break through her introverted mask and uncover
the real Kate Holmes, not the girl her mother had no
doubt taught her to be.

It took the entire trip before I got her to laugh. But
when she accepted my invitation for a personal grand
tour, something told me the hardest part was over. When
we landed on the island, the hydrofoil threading its way
through a maze of junks and fishing vessels, I escorted
her down the gangplank and into a waiting pedicab. It
was a combination rickshaw and bicycle, just built for two
and perfect for seeing the sights.

And just as I'd promised, I gave her the royal treatment, from the Camoens Gardens with its fancifully po-
etic grotto, to the ruins of the ancient Cathedral of St.
Paul, Macao's most famous landmark. Together we stood
within a hundred yards of the Portas do Cerco, the barrier gate which separates the peninsula from Communist
China. On one side of the arch flew the red and green
standard of Portugal. Atop the other side of the barrier
the five-starred red flag of Mao's China billowed proudly.
No photographs were permitted.

"I wonder what goes on behind there," Kate said, pointing to the red flag.

"Your guess is as good as mine." I meant it, too.

Lunch at the Pousada De Macau, the Macao Inn, finally did the trick, completely obliterating the last of her reserve. A fine old Portuguese rosé helped loosen her tongue as we went from crabmeat and asparagus soup to prawns à la Macanese, to apple and banana fritters with egg-nog sauce. All through lunch she kept up a steady stream of conversation, liberally spiced with laughter. And when we finally hit the casinos later that afternoon, Marian Librarian had disappeared into the stacks, hopefully never to be seen or heard from again.

"I can't begin to tell you what an absolutely wonderful day I've had, Josh," she said as we strolled leisurely down the Avenida Almeida Ribiero, past gold and ocher villas, pedicabs cycling slowly by on either side.

"It isn't over yet. How about dinner tonight? I just have some business to take care of," I said, thinking of the passport I had to pick up before the Consulate closed. "Then I'm free for the rest of the evening."

"Just dinner?" she asked, a little bit hesitant, a little bit virginal.

"Scout's honor," I promised, raising one hand to my heart.

She smiled and nodded her head. "You've got yourself a date, Mr. Morley," she announced, surprising me even more when she leaned forward, stood on tiptoe, and kissed me lightly on the cheek.

I couldn't knock it. At least it was a step in the right direction.

A moment later Kate was clinging to my arm, her tawny blonde head dropping softly against my shoulder. I pulled her closer, stopped in the middle of the broad, spacious avenue and turned to face her. She raised her eyes, come-hither as opposed to your-books-are-overdue, and let me do the honors. She had a mouth that drew me even nearer, not content until I was nibbling on her lips, my hands around her shoulders and her body pressed tightly against me.

"Not here," I heard her say, flushing with embarrassment. It might have been the oldest line in the book, but somehow it rang true, as genuine as her slim young body, as desirable as her soft pliant lips.

Threading her arm through mine, Kate now seemed perfectly content to let me lead her back to the waiting hydrofoil. The dock swarmed with peasants and tourists, but since we had our reservations and round-trip tickets, we didn't have any difficulty re-claiming our seats.

The South China Sea had turned choppy and steel-gray. The coast of mainland China was covered in a scrim of dense mist and spume thrown up by the breaking white-caps. We slipped slowly out of the harbor and Kate once again leaned against me and closed her eyes. "Too much excitement," I whispered in her ear. "You can take the girl out of Wisconsin, but you can't take Wisconsin out of the girl."

She neither agreed nor disagreed, already half-asleep.

Well, all I can say is, Carter couldn't have been more content. At least for the first ten or fifteen minutes of the return voyage.

I was looking forward to the evening which lay ahead, when something—some*one*, actually—insinuated himself into my field of vision and then my thoughts. A shadow first of annoyance and then trepidation cast its pall across my mind. Out of the corner of my eye I saw one of the other passengers, a man of nondescript appearance save for a pair of narrowed and inquiring black eyes. These were directed at me, and with far more than just casual or even friendly interest.

You're imagining things, I told myself. Just because nothing's happened to spoil your day, your eyes are playing tricks on you.

But no, that kind of simple rationalization just didn't work. Whenever I turned my head to the side, there was that same pair of darting and inquisitive black eyes, always sliding away the moment I connected with them. It

was like a game of cat and mouse, and I had no intention
of ending up as someone's dinner.

"Excuse me a sec," I murmured to Kate as I got up from
my seat.

Dazed, drunk on the briny sea air, she opened her eyes
for all of ten seconds. "Where're you going?" she asked,
her voice no louder than a whisper.

"Nature calls," I said and smiled gamely as I slipped
past her. I didn't look back, didn't wait to see if the man
who had been watching me was now going to follow as I
made my way belowdecks to the men's room. I could feel
the hard unyielding bulge of Wilhelmina, the Luger secure
within my shoulder holster. I could feel Hugo's soft
chamois sheath rubbing against the inside of my arm,
ready to be revealed by a mere flick of the wrist. And if
those two helpmates wouldn't be enough, there was always Pierre, freshly charged, attached to my upper thigh
and eager to join me in battle.

Hopefully, there wouldn't be a need for all or any of
them.

Hopefully, I was just being paranoid, super-cautious,
not about to let my technique slide, my defenses become
sloppy, slipshod.

More than likely the man who'd been staring at me had
been turned on by Kate, plain and simple. But I had to find
out for sure, one way or the other. I went down a flight of
metal stairs, then along a narrow corridor, and I pushed
open a door marked GENTS, English on one line, Cantonese on the next. A quick discreet inspection revealed
an empty lavatory, nothing to arouse my suspicions. An
oversized rectangular mirror fronted three stainless-steel
sinks. I turned on the hot water tap and slowly and me-
thodically washed my hands, keeping my eyes glued to
the mirror, to the reflection of the swinging door which led
in and out of the men's room.

I was using a wad of paper toweling with judicious
speed when my vigilance was finally rewarded. With a

faint rush of air, the door swung silently open to admit a sauntering, tight-lipped figure. It was the same passenger who had been watching me from his seat, back on deck. Not a word was spoken. Ever so slowly, my fingers moved towards my shoulder holster, even as the man sidled up to the sink and began to go through the same mundane operation which I had just completed.

He scrubbed his hands as though he were on his way to an operating theater, never once turning his eyes in my direction. I didn't say a word, didn't do a thing to interfere. Wilhelmina was within easy reach and that was all the reassurance I needed. I was wondering if he was about to offer me a hot Seiko watch or perhaps a wide assortment of dirty postcards, when the reflection I was studying in the glass finally broke its vow of silence.

"I believe," he announced, his voice pitched so low I had to strain to hear him, "that we have a friend in common, Mr. Morley."

The two KGB agents knew me as Morley, as did the late Poy Chu. "Do we really?" I said, allowing just a hint of sarcasm to creep into my voice.

"Yes," the man replied, still going through the ritual of washing and drying his slim, boyish hands. "A fellow worker of mine entrusted me with some information, Mr. Morley—some very important information, I believe."

"What's your fellow worker's name?"

"He used to be called Poy Chu," the man said, snickering softly as though his words were supposed to provoke mirth, not apprehension. "Of course, I understand that now he is not his usual talkative self. Is that not the case, Mr. Morley?"

I turned slowly to the side to face him. He was doing a good job of keeping his hands out in the open, right where I could see them, perhaps fearing he'd end up as uncommunicative as his late co-worker. "You know as much as I do," I told him, taking in his measure in a single all-encompassing glance. He was a thin, slight man in his early thirties, but there was a wiry quality to him which put me on my guard. Even if I had Wilhelmina, Hugo and Pierre, plus the benefit of a good fifty pounds, he might just show himself to be my match, particularly if he was well-acquainted with the martial arts. And that was something I just didn't want to chance or take for granted. So I was necessarily cautious and wary, despite the fact that he was doing nothing, absolutely nothing, to provoke an attack.

"Yes, he is no longer ... talkative," he finally replied, using a last paper towel to dry his hands. "Very sad, but perhaps he was careless, my old friend Poy Chu. But as I said, Mr. Morley, I now have the information you require. I am sure that must please you."

"It might," I said, hedging my bets until I knew for sure if he was straight, the person he claimed to be. "It depends on the information."

"Oh, it is most excellent information," he affirmed.

"Concerning?"

"Pardon?"

"I said, what kind of information do you have to give me?"

"Not *give* you, Mr. Morley," he corrected with a cryptic grin. "*Sell* you. I believe that is the correct way to speak it. Phrase it, right?"

Two hundred thousand was still sitting in the Hong Kong & Shanghai Bank, back in Victoria. Needless to say, I wasn't about to part with a penny of it until Poy Chu's self-styled "friend" told me what it was he had to offer. "I was prepared to pay Poy Chu," I said, "and I'll be just as prepared to pay you, once I know what I'm buying."

The man curled his lips back, exposing two even rows of small, sparkling white teeth. "It concerns a most important document," he said. "But now is wrong time for explanation, discussion."

I could feel the hydrofoil cutting through the water,

rocking ever so gently from starboard to port and back again. The engine hum vibrated in my ears. "Now is the best possible time," I replied. "We have all the privacy we require."

The man glanced at the swinging door and then back in my direction. "Not true," he said.

"What do you mean?" my eyes narrowing with curiosity.

"We are both being watched, Mr. Morley," he explained, choosing his words with what struck me as the utmost of care and delicacy.

"Watched?" I exclaimed. "By whom?"

"By someone who is, shall we say, a good friend of the Peking government."

The mysterious third party who had cut Poy Chu's throat? I thought to myself. Or perhaps even a fourth party? But there was still no way of knowing, not when Poy Chu's fellow worker continued to remain taciturn, stubbornly refusing to explain himself or go into detail.

"You must know by now you have been followed all the time you are in Hong Kong," he told me. "They know how you move, what you do. Even now, today," he said, and for some inexplicable reason he suddenly thumped himself on the chest, hitting his sternum with a hollow drumlike sound, "they wait for you to lead them to . . . Poy Chu's information, shall we say."

"And you know where that information is?"

"That is correct, Mr. Morley."

"And you know who's been following me?"

"That too is correct."

"Then who is it?"

The man smiled broadly, amused by my steady stream of questions. He opened his mouth and suddenly slumped forward against the stainless-steel sink. Even as I saw his astonished black eyes roll up in his head to expose yellowish whites, I was throwing myself flat out against the floor. I hit the checkered tiles without a pause, without a moment of reflection, indecision. My actions were totally instinctive, one reflex piled automatically on top of another. I had Wilhelmina in my hand, all eyes to the lavatory door which was only now swinging silently shut on its well-oiled hinges. As for Poy Chu's friend, he was now an ex-friend, slowly sinking down along the edge of the sink until he fell in a dead and bloody heap at my feet.

Gingerly, I picked myself up off the floor, got shakily to my feet and raced towards the swinging door, Wilhelmina in hand. I eased the door open and peered cautiously out into the narrow corridor. It was deserted, the assassin seemingly having vanished into thin air. There was no way I could make a thorough search of the vessel, not with over a hundred other passengers to contend with. I turned around and slipped back into the men's room.

A wet scarlet blossom had already spread across the man's starched white shirt front. His lips were parted, an expression of surprise and disbelief, printed across his face. It seemed as if he had never expected to be picked off so neatly, seemingly without effort. Up on deck, or somewhere on the hydrofoil, someone with a silencer was no doubt quite satisfied, having performed precisely the way Peking had instructed.

I had to work fast, lest one of the other passengers decide to make a pit stop and discover me hunched over a corpse. I went through the man's pockets as quickly as I could and was rewarded with a Hong Kong passport bearing the name of Wai Tsang.

The late Wai Tsang, I thought bitterly to myself.

But even more important than the man's identity was the fact that on the last page of his passport I discovered a freshly stamped Burmese visa, dated as recently as the day before. The long shot I had decided to chance no longer seemed half as long as it once had, nor half as farfetched or improbable.

There were no other papers on him, and certainly not the roll of microfilm. I dragged Wai Tsang's body toward the cubicles at the opposite end of the lavatory, propped him up against a seat and locked the door from the inside. Then I climbed over the partition, cleaned the blood off the floor and left the john as surreptitiously as I could. If Kate asked what had taken me so long, I would tell her "Montezuma's revenge," Asian style.

In any event, it had now become apparent that party or parties unknown were quite convinced I would be able to lead them directly to the microfilm. So for the time being at least, I was far more valuable alive than dead.

Somehow, it wasn't as comforting as it sounded.

CHAPTER FIVE

DAY ONE—first day of seven allowed by the Burmese government.

I was aboard a UBA—Union of Burma Airways— flight, nonstop from Hong Kong's Kai Tak International to Mingaladon Airport, fifteen miles outside the Rangoon city limits. All four stews, two in the fore cabin and two in the aft, were decked out in native costume, multi-colored sarongs, *longyi,* over which they wore marvelously sheer and diaphanous blouses. These all but transparent garments were known as *ingyi.* Despite considerable expenditures of time and money, the Burmese government had been unable to legislate against them, even after attaching such words a decadent, lewd, and lascivious. Women were women the world over; no one was going to tell them what they could and could not wear.

The stewardesses were no different.

Their long, silken black hair was bound up, high against the nape of their necks. Their small pear-shaped breasts moved seductively as they threaded their way up and down the center aisle, eager to please, eager to demonstrate what I hoped would be indicative of Burmese hospitality. They were the one comfort, visual and otherwise, in what had fast become a most uncomfortable series of events.

Can't you stay another day, Josh? she said, snuggling up against me. Why do you have to run off when ... you

*know, when we're finally getting better acquainted. Used
to each other.*

I hadn't told Kate I was headed for Burma. If anything, I'd tried to tell as few lies as possible, keeping de-
ceit to a minimum. According to what she'd said, she
didn't plan to arrive in Burma for several days. Hopefully,
I'd already be out of the country by then, microfilm in
hand.

It's funny, she said.

What is?

*You're really the first man I ever trusted, ever ... felt
safe with. I always had this image of myself as sort of the
shy, helpless type.*

Shy yes, I said with a laugh. Helpless, never.

*Never? and her bright blue eyes opened wide, taking
me in with a single eager glance.*

*Never, I repeated. My lips slid down to lick the hollow
between her neck and shoulder. My hands moved deftly,
exploring, arousing. She strained beneath me, neither coy
nor circumspect. Then she pushed upwards and met my
advance with a soft, hungry whimper of pleasure, mounting excitement. Beyond the drawn curtains, Hong Kong
dazzled the eye with an explosion of neon. I was sorry I
had to leave her, more sorry than she probably even realized.*

"Is everything satisfactory, sir?" the stewardess asked,
awakening me from my beautiful reverie, a lingering
vision of raw and unbridled passion.

"Fine," I said, knowing then that Kate had meant
much more than just a physical release. "Couldn't be better."

She smiled and turned away with a rustle of silk, leaving me alone with my thoughts. But there was work to do.
Kate Holmes would just have to take a back seat. I had
no other choice, not when my mission had barely started,
not when the roll of microfilm was yet to be found. And
even if I did succeed in locating it, there was still the

problem of smuggling it out of Burma. Perhaps I was being watched even now, though none of the other passengers gave any indication of taking more than a cursory interest in me. But still, I had no way of knowing, since the identity of party or parties unknown was precisely that, unknown, one big fat zero.

I can't say I was happy, or cocksure of myself, either.

It was late afternoon when I arrived at the National Museum. Phayre Street consisted of a narrow, unpaved lane, right off the more substantial and bustling Shwe Dagon Pagoda Road. It was here that the Cultural Institute had been established more than twenty years before. Along with the museum, the complex of buildings housed the National Gallery of Art, the National Library; and the National Academy of Music, Drama and Dancing.

I glanced back down the length of deserted street. No one left a cloud of dust in their wake. No one darted into the shadows. I was alone, at least for the time being. Passing through one entrance, one which was marked Ministry of Union Culture, I proceeded up three flights of marble stairs until I reached the museum proper. The famous Lion Throne, returned to Burma by the British in 1964, stood right inside the second set of doors. Impressive as it was, I was looking for something of an entirely different period and from a different culture as well.

It was then that I saw the printed notices, written in both Burmese and English. The exhibit of Han Dynasty artifacts had just opened that very morning. I turned right, passed through two halls and a gallery housing the museum's collection of Mandalay court regalia, and finally arrived before a uniformed guard, attired in Western as opposed to Burmese costume.

After paying the small admission fee, I slipped inside and headed directly to the central display, eager to see Tou Wan's jade funerary suit. It was ringed by wine-colored velvet ropes and another uniformed guard was stationed at the foot of the glass and wood-framed case. Before now, I'd only seen a photograph of the death suit. One look, and I knew it hadn't done it any justice at all.

Dazzling was the only word for the blue-green burial armor. The jade plaques were crosshatched in gold and linked with wire that was also of the same gleaming yellow metal. Though nothing remained of the Han princess save for the armor itself, you could almost feel her presence—imperious and aloof—there in that gallery of hushed voices and whispered comments. Perhaps a dozen other visitors moved slowly about the exhibit, most of them Westerners, tourists no doubt. But I wasn't interested in the other artifacts which were also part of the traveling display.

No, I had eyes only for Tou Wan's death suit, and nothing else.

Somewhere within that life-sized suit of jade armor, I was certain Poy Chu—or one of his confederates back in Peking—had secreted a roll of film, film which I had to locate before my seven-day visa expired. But needless to say, it was impossible to make a search of the case and its invaluable contents until the museum was emptied of guards and visitors alike.

I glanced warily around, trying to determine if someone was watching me, dogging my tracks. But no one, save for the guard who stood alongside the testament to Tou Wan's vanity, seemed to notice me or take any interest in my presence.

I looked back at him, flashed a polite smile, and asked if I might be able to speak to the curator in charge of the exhibit. "No English," he said, shaking his head.

"Won ne par de," I began again, rephrasing the question in his native Burmese. *"Chay-zoo pyu-pah . . ."*

It took awhile to get my message across, but finally he grinned, obviously quite pleased I knew his language, or at least enough to make myself understood. He directed me to the opposite end of the gallery, thence to a narrow corridor lined with offices.

"Ask for Mr. Aung Nu."

Unfortunately, it wasn't as easy as all that. When I reached the far end of the exhibit hall, my path was blocked by yet another uniformed attendant. Either the Burmese or the Chinese or both weren't taking any chances. They had the place staked out as though they were exhibiting the Kohinoor diamond.

"No allowing," he said, which sort of went hand in glove with the signs I'd noticed near the Shwe Dagon: "Footwearing is prohibited."

"Mr. Aung Nu," I said.

"No allowing," he repeated, giving me the grimmest expression in his repertoire.

"Aung Nu," I said for the third time.

Perhaps it was my persistence, or perhaps just my tone of voice. But the guard finally acquiesced, motioning me on with an outstretched finger and directed right behind him. I found the curator's office without further difficulty. A brisk and official knock and the door opened to reveal the owl-eyed figure of Aung Nu. He blinked rapidly at me from behind his wire-rimmed eyeglasses, a questioning expression settling just as quickly across his face.

"May I help you?" he asked, his English as impeccable as his manners.

"I hope so," I said, introducing myself a moment later. "I'm quite taken with your exhibit, Mr. Aung Nu. Oriental art, particularly of the Han Dynasty period, has always held a special fascination for me. And I must say I've never seen such an impressive collection as this one, and all under one roof."

"I am glad you are enjoying the exhibit," he said, smiling.

"Oh yes, very much so. Tou Wan's burial suit is a most brilliant achievement—remarkable." I clucked my tongue, histrionic and emphatic. "And as for the T'ang horseman which I understand was found at Ch'iensien, such artistry and craftsmanship, such a synthesis of form and movement, have rarely been seen before," I continued, laying on the charm and erudition as much as possible.

"Please," he said, beckoning me inside with a wave of his hand. "Won't you please take a seat. It is not often I am in the company of a man of your ... aesthetic appreciation—sophistication shall we say."

"I am honored, Mr. Aung Nu."

The door closed behind us.

It was a smiling Nick Carter who emerged from the curator's "humble digs"—as he himself had described his cubby-hole of an office, half an hour later. Mr. Aung Nu would be joining me for dinner. In fact, he couldn't have been more delighted to be my guest. I hoped it didn't have anything to do with the fact that good restaurants were at a premium in Rangoon, all but nonexistent ever since the anti-Chinese riots of 1967. Nevertheless, my thoughts were far removed from gourmet treats and epicurean delicacies, Southeast Asian or otherwise. Without his realizing it, without making Aung Nu aware of what I was doing, I fully intended to pump him for as much information as I possibly could. That meant everything from a floor plan to the placement of guards, from the location of entrances and exits to a complete review of the museum's security system.

Things were turning out better than I would have expected.

And dinner, early that evening, only gave me cause for optimism, if not out-and-out celebration. The dining room of the Strand Hotel, a stone's throw from the Rangoon River, served as a fitting backdrop for our second and exceedingly cordial meeting. Amid the dusty palms and Victorian statuary, the hum of overhead fans and obsequious waiters—all the paraphernalia and appurtenances of British colonialism circa 1937—Aung Nu smiled and chatted, chatted and smiled. Not only affable, he was extremely talkative, as well.

"You know," he said, accepting my offer of a cigar and brandy after the dishes—chipped but serviceable—had been cleared, "this has been a great cultural coup for the museum. After all, relations with the People's Republic of China are yet to be stabilized. So the loan of the Han artifacts is a display of good feeling between the Chinese and our own people. Too bad so few residents of Rangoon have been attracted to the exhibit. I fear it might just be that anti-Chinese sentiments are yet to . . . dissipate?" He looked at me questioningly.

"Yes, dissipate," I said, my mind on other things entirely. "No doubt they've sent their own security team, to travel with the exhibit, that is."

Aung Nu shook his head, savored his brandy, and leaned back in his seat. Luxuriating in the atmosphere of faded opulence, he went on to tell me that the government had refused to allow armed Chinese into the country. "So we must do all the security work ourselves," he explained. "It is not so very difficult. Our citizens here in Rangoon are not particularly interested in antiquities. No one goes hungry, but people spend many nights out on the streets. There is just not enough housing . . . yes, that is the correct way of putting it, Mr. Morley. Just not enough adequate housing to meet our national needs."

"A most unhappy situation," I said, commiserating with him even as I steered the conversation back in a direction I was far more anxious to explore. "I suppose you use the American system . . ."

"I don't believe I know what that system is," the curator replied, as charmingly ingenuous as he'd been all evening.

We'd already covered opening and closing hours, alarm networks, exits and entrances. Now, I wanted to know exactly how many guards would be on duty while the rest of Rangoon was asleep. "Staggered hours," I said, bluffing my way to the facts I needed to know. "For example, at our famous Museum of Modern Art in New York City, they employ two dozen guards from closing until midnight, and then half as many from midnight until six a.m."

"Oh, now I understand," he said and nodded his head and took another swallow of brandy. "But no, we cannot afford such elaborate precautions, nor do we have the funds to employ so many attendants."

"So you make do with what you have, I take it?"

"Exactly. Between one and six in the morning, the museum is all but empty. But let us talk about the recent discoveries at Ch'angsha."

Fortunately, I'd done my homework. I knew exactly what he was referring to. "You are, of course, speaking of the tomb of Lady Hsin Chui."

"Of course," he said and smiled broadly, pleased with my knowledge.

"I was most excited by the *fei i,* the flying garment which described the legendary exploits of Ch'ang O."

"Yes indeed," he concurred with another expression of satisfaction. "It is a most remarkable artifact. It was Ch'ang O, you remember, who stole the elixir of immortality, taking flight on a dragon's wings—"

"Speaking of dragon's wings, is there any way a girl can get a hot meal around here?"

I jerked my head over my shoulder, frowned and smiled in rapid succession, and got hastily to my feet.

Kate Holmes extended her hand. "Surprise," she said with a girlish little laugh.

It might very well prove to be the understatement of this or any other year.

CHAPTER SIX

I recovered my composure seconds later. "Mr. Aung Nu, Ms. Katherine Holmes, a friend of mine."

"I am honored," he said, standing and bowing his head slightly.

The two of us remained standing until Kate had taken a seat. I motioned to the captain with a wave of my hand. After he had taken her order and after the waiter had re-filled our coffee cups, I settled back and eyed her curiously. Dressed in a khaki safari suit, her honey-blonde hair no longer tied up in a bun, she was even more attractive than when I'd last seen her, less than twenty-four hours before.

"You look like the cat who swallowed the canary, Josh," she said with another gay and infectious laugh. She turned towards the curator. "Joshua and I met in Hong Kong, Mr. Aung Nu. I'm on my way to Pagan to do some field work, and I'm afraid he never told me he was headed for Burma. It's a small world, even if that does sound like a cliché."

"Very small," Aung Nu said, grinning first at me and then at Kate. "But how pleasant a surprise it must be for the two of you."

"Very," I said, scowling behind my smile. I hadn't wanted Kate around, lest her presence complicate things for me. As recently as a year before, less even, precisely that kind of unforeseen—unwanted, too—incident had taken place, while I was en route to Katmandu. The result had not been a very happy one. I'd met a young woman, Andrea Yuen, on my way over to Amsterdam. One thing had led to another and another had led to a bullet which put her in intensive care for more than a month. I didn't want to see a repetition of that kind of carelessness.

"But Josh," she said, subtly protesting my lack of enthusiasm, "it's not all that surprising. After all, the Strand is the only first-class hotel in Rangoon."

"There's always the Inya Lake," I said, referring to the Russian-built hotel on the outskirts of the capital.

"It's so poorly maintained," she replied. "And besides, this way I'm within walking distance of the Shwe Dagon, and the outdoor market. But I don't know why I'm sitting here making apologies. I told you I was on my way to Burma, when we first met. You didn't tell me you intended to stop here."

"I must be going," Aung Nu said, getting abruptly to his feet as though he feared being a party to an altercation. "Mr. Morley, it was a most enjoyable evening. If you plan to return visit to the museum, I would be very disappointed if you did not stop by to say hello."

"I won't forget," I assured him, shaking his hand. "You've helped make my stay a memorable one. It's not often I find myself in such knowledgeable company."

Visibly blushing, he made his good-byes to Kate and took his leave. We were alone in the middle of the all but deserted dining room. Rangoon was not what one would call a bustling tourist center.

"Well, I'm sorry you're angry." She looked down at her plate, as petulant and sulky as a spoiled child.

"I'm not angry," I protested. "Anger doesn't have anything to do with it. I'm just . . . surprised and pleased and a little bit out of breath. Now how's that for honesty?" I reached for her hand, gave it an affectionate squeeze, and glossed over my obvious discomfort.

No, it really wasn't a surprise she'd turned up at the

Strand. If anything, my presence in Rangoon smacked of the unexpected, not hers.

"Why didn't you tell me you were coming here?" she asked, finally condescending to raise her eyes off her plate.

"I really didn't think we'd be able to rework our schedules, that's why," I lied. "So I just kept my mouth shut. You're the one who arrived early, when you get right down to it."

"Hong Kong just wasn't the same without you, Mr. Morley." She laughed at what I imagined she considered a most brazen remark.

It wasn't. It was charming.

And it was even more charming when, less than an hour later, we picked up where we had last left off in Kowloon. Bathed in the soft amber light of her bedside lamp, Kate looked more desirable than ever. Behind her thin and clinging peignoir, her skin was flushed, her firm outthrust breasts swaying with delicate insistence. I reached for the ribbon tie which would undo her night-gown, but she stepped nimbly back, a playful smile creasing the corners of her lips.

"You're a very strange man, Joshua. Very ... how shall I put it? Very mysterious."

"Do you find that exciting?"

She nodded her head. "Yes. It ... it turns me on. Isn't that silly?"

"No, not if it pleases you."

"It does, Josh, really it does." She came to me then, slid down onto the bed to press against my side. Her fingers wandered slowly across my chest, tugged at the wiry hair, then moved lower, lower still. A groan of excitement escaped my lips. I thrust my hips up, met her languorous fingers and pressed them down against my hard and straining sex.

It was her turn to groan. I heard her give a soft and strangled little cry as I pushed her head down, urging her around so that one pleasure would invite another. She was more than willing to do exactly as I wished, if only because there was nothing selfish in the way we found ourselves entangled, arms and legs twisted heatedly about each other. A hot musky scent rose up in the air like a tropical perfume, only to blend imperceptibly into the sultry Burmese night.

She gave another hoarse whimper of pleasure and then we were moving as one.

Hours later, my Rolex glowing 12:15, I eased myself off the bed and dressed in the darkness. I had business to take care of, business which could not be put off any longer. Aung Nu had said that few guards were on duty after one A.M. I held him to his word, left Kate sound asleep, and returned to my room to collect my equipment. Then, making use of a service entrance I had noticed earlier in the day, I slipped out of the hotel, unnoticed and unobserved.

Beneath the streetlamps, clouds of gnats and tiny flying insects reeled in dense and choking swarms. Passing beneath them on my way down the Strand Road, I could feel the bugs getting entangled in my hair, flying into my mouth, filling my nostrils. I slammed my eyelids shut and broke into a run, brushing at my face.

The night was alive with the whisper of voices. Entire families lay stretched out on grass mats, claiming their sidewalk's share of sleeping space. I walked in the middle of the street, not a single headlight catching me as I hurried through the darkness.

From the Strand Road I moved north, past Merchant, Dalhousie, Fraser, and Bogyoke Streets. Everywhere it was the same. Small fires cast flickering shadows along the facades of shabby buildings the British had left behind. Curious-eyed faces, transient and homeless, turned to follow me as I made my way towards Phayre Street and the National Museum.

I had been in strange places before, backwaters, countries which had forgotten the twentieth century. I'd spent whole weeks with the mudmen of New Guinea, the Dyaks of Malaysia, primitive tribesmen living equally primitive lives. But nowhere in all my travels had I felt the collapse of the West as I did in Rangoon. Nothing seemed to have changed since the British had departed nearly thirty years before. Everywhere I turned I had the same sinking sensation—a feeling of being smothered in decay, obsolescence, defeat.

It didn't do wonders for my morale, that's for sure.

Twenty or so minutes of a jogging pace and countless backward glances put me at the corner of Shwe Dagon Pagoda Road and Phayre Street. I stopped to catch my breath, to double-check that no one was on my tail, dogging my tracks. Satisfied that I hadn't been followed, I turned onto Phayre Street and silently made my way to the Ministry of Union Culture. Needless to say, the front doors were locked. But I wasn't about to give up so easily, not when Tou Wan's jade death suit might very well be concealing a roll of microfilm that was as irreplaceable as it was invaluable.

Skirting the front of the museum, I moved cautiously around to the back. A narrow, unpaved alley, one that reeked of garbage, was all that separated the Ministry from an adjacent building. Both were equally as silent, equally as nondescript. Using my pocket flashlight, I sent a narrow high-intensity beam skittering across the base of the Cultural Institute. A row of basement windows, each one covered with a screen of wire mesh, was revealed in the glow of my torch. I flicked off the light, crouched down in front of the first of four identical windows, and probed the screen with my fingers.

The blade of a pocketknife was quickly brought into play. I pried off the screen and felt around for the window latch. There wasn't any. The window was locked from the inside, which meant that I would have to break the glass in order to gain access to the museum, three stories above me. Wadding my handkerchief around my fist, I held my breath and slammed my hand across the glass. The linen handkerchief absorbed both the pain and some of the noise. The glass shattered, tinkling softly. A moment later I found the latch I'd been searching for. Gingerly, careful not to cut myself against the shards of broken glass, I slid it free and pushed down along the bottom edge of the window. The wooden frame creaked in protest, as if it hadn't been opened in years. I applied pressure once again, careful to make as little noise as possible. Finally, the window slid back.

I had no idea where it would lead to, Aung Nu's verbal floor plan leaving much to be desired. But it was time I found out, and so I eased myself through the narrow opening, feetfirst.

That was the easy part.

But when it came to my shoulders, I felt like a sardine packed in a tin. It was a tight fit, too tight for comfort. I let go of the window frame and pushed my left arm through and then my right, ducked my head, and slid down until both feet touched ground. When I straightened up again, the darkness was still as thick and impenetrable as it had been when I'd first broken the window. I couldn't see in front of me and so I eased the window down and pulled out my flashlight. Aung Nu hadn't mentioned anything about watchmen being on duty outside the museum. Still, I realized I was taking a chance, a calculated risk. Hopefully, if my luck would hold out, no one would come upon the broken window, at least not until after I had left the museum and made good my escape.

The high-intensity beam was like a mote of sunlight, cloudy with swirling particles of dust. I was aware of a dank, musty scent, an aroma that conjured up attics and haunted houses, airless and close. No wonder, because it didn't take very long before I figured out that I'd landed in a storeroom of sorts, one that was filled with all manner of dusty bric-a-brac. Fragments of pottery, pieces of broken statuary, stone lions and innumerable Buddhas, were all revealed as I swung the flashlight from one side of the storeroom to the other.

Hintha Gong was there as well, a carved representation of the mythical bird which rose from the sea. Behind the wooden statue, which must have been a hundred years old if not more, lacquered bowls were piled helter-skelter, reaching halfway to the ceiling. I threaded my way through the archaeological debris until I came to the door which led out of the storeroom and into another section of the damp and dust-clogged basement.

The door was locked.

Not that I'd expected it to swing back at the mention of "open sesame." But still, it only complicated things, particularly since I was trying my damnedest to be as silent as possible. Nevertheless, I'd come prepared for all contingencies, or as many as I'd been able to think of in advance. From my inside breast pocket I removed a paper-thin square of acetate. It was an old burglar's trick, one I now put quickly to use. Wedging the plastic sheet between the door and the jamb, I slid it slowly down past the lock. The first time it didn't work, but I wasn't about to give up so easily.

Once again I eased the acetate square between the two wooden surfaces, felt it hit the rusty metal lock, then, pushed down with slightly more force than before. A soft click was my reward, that and a doorknob which now turned with a creak and a rasp. Silent, watchful, I let myself out of the storeroom and peered out. A wide corridor, one whose ceiling revealed a complex of hot and cold water pipes, ran parallel to the basement storage room. I shut the door softly behind me and turned right.

So far, so good.

The hallway ended abruptly less than fifty feet later. An old and creaking wooden staircase joined up with the basement corridor. I gripped the bannister and took the steps one at a time, craning my neck to see if anyone was waiting for me at the top of the landing. No one was. I passed the first floor without encountering anything more significant than a rat. Its reddish eyes glowed in the darkness as it scurried past me, hugging the wall.

I proceeded up the next flight of stairs, even more cautiously than before. Again, no one stopped me, verbally or otherwise. A few minutes later I reached the landing which led out onto the third floor of the Cultural Institute, the floor which housed both the collection of the National Museum and the Han Dynasty exhibit.

The metal safety door, the one modern feature I'd encountered so far, was unlocked. I pushed down against the bar and the door swung open enough to allow me to slip inside. The poured concrete of the landing was immediately replaced by first parquet and then marble. I waited silently by the door, my eyes adjusting to the diminished light. Up ahead I could see the display of Mandalay court regalia, enabling me to get my bearings without further difficulty.

I would have to make my way through that gallery before I reached the hall where the traveling exhibit was being displayed. There were plenty of museum cases to serve as needed cover, but I wasn't so foolish as to think I could merely saunter down the hall and pass unseen from one exhibit room to the next. No, everything had to be done as invisibly as possible. Failure just wasn't in the vocabulary of my mission.

At least it wasn't as dark as it had been back in the storeroom, or even on the stairs. Several low-wattage bulbs glowed fitfully at the opposite end of the corridor. I waited in the shadows. My Rolex read a phosphorescent and optimistic 1:09. My timing wasn't off and now I hoped nothing else would be, either. Finally, I took the first step towards what I hoped would end in complete and total success, the recovery of the spy list, my safe passage out of Burma, and then straight to Dupont Circle and the Director and Operations Chief of AXE. Only when Hawk had the film in his hands would I give myself the luxury of breathing a sigh of relief.

I reached the entrance to the Mandalay gallery, only to hear footfalls echoing softly at the other end of the hall. A museum case provided the necessary cover. I ducked out of sight, crouched down and waited. The footsteps grew louder, leather against marble, regular and evenly spaced. Judging from his unhurried stride, the guard wasn't acting as though he were either alarmed or suspicious, which was just the way I wanted things to remain.

A lean, sallow-faced man in his late twenties walked slowly down the central corridor between the rows of glass and wood cases. He was less than fifteen feet away from me as I stayed out of sight, unable to ignore the bulging black leather holster he wore along his hip, that and the rounded butt end of a Colt .38. It was a Police Positive Special, a handgun whose double-action mechanism would make it all too easy for the guard to get off six rounds without breaking his stride, without having to bother about manually cocking the revolver's hammer.

It was one fact which Aung Nu had neglected to mention, one fact which I, in turn, had neglected to ask. It also made me twice as wary and doubly alert. Despite the fact that there were supposedly no more than half a dozen men on duty at this hour of the night, apparently they were exceedingly well-armed. The rest of Rangoon may have resembled a shabby movie set for a thirties spy thriller, but the museum watchmen were outfitted circa 1975, toting the best sidearms money could buy.

I waited in the shadows until the guard had left the gallery. Only then did I make my way along the narrow aisle, keeping as close to the wall as I could. A grandiose marble arch met my eye, then the upright rectangle of a makeshift ticket stand, and finally ...

Sonuvabitch, I swore to myself, even as I ducked back out of sight.

White suit and Eastern Europe had beat me to the

punch. They were one up on me, hard at work trying to remove the glass cover of the museum case in which Tou Wan's jade death suit had been carefully arrayed. Several yards to the left of the case, two guards lay sprawled out across the floor, unconscious. But even as I watched British accent and his hefty sidekick—both pinkies swathed in bandages like worm-sized mummies—I realized their presence would be less troublesome than I'd first thought.

Let them do the dirty work for me, I thought to myself. After all, I have Wilhelmina. She's ready whenever I am.

They must have just gotten there, because the last guard I'd seen had been coming from the direction of the Han Dynasty exhibit. Now, both men worked in absolute silence, not a word of English—or Russian, for that matter—passing between their lips. As for the glass cover, it was giving them more difficulty than I would have imagined. Making use of a variety of small tools, they sought to separate it from the polished wooden base, a kind of platform upon which the funerary armor had been laid out.

I looked back, covering the Mandalay gallery with a single all-encompassing sweep of my eyes. It was empty. When I turned back to watch the two men I still assumed were agents sent by the deadly KGB, they had finally succeeded in prying off one end of the glass cover.

"Slowly," I heard white suit hiss between his teeth.

His partner nodded his head, worked a screwdriver under the side of the glass and pushed down. The wood creaked, the glass lid jerked back and forth and finally parted from the base of the case.

"Careful," white suit muttered. He took hold of one end of the cover while Eastern Europe managed to get a grip on the other end. Together, they lifted the transparent top of the museum case and raised it up a good foot above the jade suit. Then they moved slowly to the side, not stopping until they cleared the burial armor.

"Now down," British accent whispered, helping his partner set the glass lid onto the marble floor.

A moment later he was pawing at the armor, lifting up one section after another in his search for the microfilm. There was no reason for me to interfere, not until he came across what he was so anxious to find. But long before either of the two men had given the burial suit the careful search and painstaking examination it required, footsteps echoed loudly from the opposite end of the Mandalay gallery.

I crept back so that the guards wouldn't be able to see me, while white suit and his broken-fingered companion hurriedly replaced the glass cover. They set it down on top of the armor and the polished wooden base of the museum case. Then darting out of sight, they concealed themselves behind an adjacent display.

The footsteps grew louder, a rhythm of uncertainty, as if the men who were approaching the Han exhibit sensed that something was not as it should be. Perhaps they were aware of the fact that two guards were missing. But whatever had induced them to return to the far gallery, they now seemed to be making up for lost time.

I could hear them speaking in anxious voices as they hurried towards the arch and ticket stand. They stopped less than six feet away from me, two hands reaching simultaneously for two high-powered Police Positive Specials. But the two unconscious attendants were evidence enough. One of the guards, the same lean and sallow-faced young man I had seen a few minutes earlier, lost no time rushing toward his fallen comrades while the second guard, his revolver drawn, stepped warily into the darkened exhibit hall.

If I didn't act now, my two Soviet counterparts might just end up as living proof that crime pays. I didn't want that to happen. There was no way was I going to allow them to get off scot-free. So without thinking twice about it, I reached into my pocket and pulled out a handful of *kyats,* thin Burmese coins that had a ring of tin to them. I knew where white suit (he was currently decked out in dapper black) and his cauliflower-eared henchman were hiding and I edged forward and tossed the coins in their direction.

The metal currency clattered like buckshot and the coins scattered and rolled across the marble floor. Both guards gave identical cries of surprise. And the moment they yelled out in alarm, the British defector (his use of English when he'd been alone with broken fingers seemed to confirm what I'd previously only assumed to be the case) and his accomplish started from their hiding place and made a mad dash for the exit at the far end of the gallery.

The two uniformed guards weren't about to let them off so easily. A shot rang out, followed by a second whine of angry lead, followed by the reverberation of a third bone-shattering slug. Eastern Europe stumbled, lost his rhythm like a colt on a wet track, then completely lost his footing.

He gave a single liquid gurgle of pain, coughed up a hefty wad of phlegm and blood, and crumpled to the floor. His partner had no intention of waiting around, watching him rattle about on the floor as he suffered his death throes. He slipped out of sight, heading down the narrow corridor where I had gone in search of Aung Nu the day before. As for the two museum guards, they didn't intend to give up so easily, either. They chased after him, getting off another round before the hall was once again deserted save for three fallen bodies, the most recent twisted into a grotesque and bloody heap.

I just didn't have the time—or inclination—to administer first aid. Besides, it was too late. Broken fingers' luck had finally run out.

I made a mental note to send a condolence card to his superiors and darted out of the shadows. I raced across the marble floor in the direction of the museum case, even as I heard additional shots ringing out, one reverberating more loudly than the next. There wasn't much time. The two guards still lying on the floor might very well come to at any moment. The two guards who had gone off in pursuit of British accent might very well return to the gallery. And there was the chance that the final pair—if not more—of armed attendants currently on duty somewhere in the museum, might come to the assistance of their comrades.

I didn't want to get caught in the cross fire.

The high-pitched drone of an alarm shattered the silence. I had to work fast, but getting a hold on the glass lid without the help of another pair of hands wasn't as easy as it looked. I kept at it until I managed to get a grip on the edge of the lid. Then I slid it back, pitched it forward, and shoved it down towards the floor. If the glass broke, I'd have everyone on my tail. So I had to be careful, despite the fact that time was fast running out.

I balanced the lid against the side of the wooden platform and went to work. The jade armor was heavier than I'd thought and it was impossible to move more than one area of the burial suit at a time. I lifted the right leg and then the left, the right arm and then its partner. I raised the head and bent the torso forward. I even picked up the *huangs and pi*, the jade crescents and disks which were arranged alongside Tou Wan's funerary suit.

But the roll of microfilm was nowhere in sight.

Someone else might have just given up, right then and there. But that's not the way I work.

Okay, I thought to myself. Where else could he have hidden it? Think, man. Where the hell would he have concealed the film?

The jade plaques were linked together with gold wire. Although the suit was hollow, it seemed highly unlikely that Poy Chu or his confederate had gone to the trouble of breaking the wire and stuffing the film inside. That kind of damage would have been noticed, even before the armor left Peking. I stuck my fingers up into the hollow plaque that served as a nasal bridge but it too proved to be empty.

Maybe the lining, I thought. Sure, why not ...

The death suit was laid out on a maroon felt backing, the color complementing the blue-green jade. I took hold of the edge of the material and began to peel it back. It was glued to a naked and unfinished surface, raw wood as opposed to the highly polished sides of the platform. Hopefully, the film had been concealed beneath the fabric and then the length of felt glued back into place.

Unfortunately, I wasn't able to get very far.

CHAPTER SEVEN

The rapid clatter of footsteps sounded above the unending drone of the alarm.

Hurriedly I pressed the felt down and grabbed hold of the edge of the glass cover. I pulled it across Tou Wan's death suit so that the case, at least at first glance, wouldn't look as though it had been disturbed.

Then I raced across the marble floor, sped past the arch and ticket stand and made it to the adjacent Mandalay gallery as loud, anxious voices rose up all around me. I caught sight of four guards, the two I'd seen previously as well as two others. But a flurry of movement at the opposite end of the hall told me there were even more armed attendants circulating on the floor, no doubt coming on the run from adjoining wings of the Cultural Institute.

The museum was fast becoming a madhouse.

I wanted out, in no uncertain terms. Keeping to the wall, I crept forward, slipping between one case and then another, all the while making sure that no one was watching my progress from one end of the gallery to the other. I figured that the safest way out would be to retrace my steps, return to the storeroom and make use of the broken window.

But as things turned out, it wasn't nearly as easy as all that.

I made it unobserved to the end of the hall, only to find the stairway blocked. If British accent had been able to elude the guards, there was no reason in the world why I couldn't. Unless of course he'd been shot or apprehended. That was something I had no way of knowing. But I did know that unless I got out of the museum, I was a sitting duck, as unpleasant a role as any I could think of.

The guard, his Colt .38 in hand, prowled back and forth before the metal safety door. A second alarm went off so that it was almost impossible to hear myself think. Pretty soon and I had a feeling an entire regiment of the Burmese army would be showing up, with or without the behest of the museum authorities. I could have picked the guard off with no trouble at all. But I didn't want to add murder to any of the other crimes I'd already committed. At this point, the attendants were aware of only two intruders, British accent and his bullet-riddled compatriot. There was no sense letting them know that a third unauthorized party was still at large, lurking somewhere in the museum.

I removed Wilhelmina from my shoulder holster, took one soundless step forward and fired off a round. The Luger's corrected hair trigger responded perfectly. A slug whistled hotly through the air, the bullet ricocheting off a marble column a good fifty feet to the right of the guard. It was a diversionary tactic, just as the coins had been. No sooner did the shot go off when the attendant threw himself down as though he'd been hit. When he realized he was still in one piece, he crept forward in the direction of the shot, leaving the staircase momentarily unguarded.

It was the "momentarily" I'd been waiting for.

No sooner did he leave his post when I made a frantic rush towards the metal door. It swung open at my touch and I heard the guard give a cry of alarm. The security sirens were muffled now as I took the stairs two and three at a time, sorry the bannisters weren't designed for sliding. Behind me came the clatter of running feet. The guard had seen me and I had to make it to the storeroom before he or one of his slugs made actual physical—as opposed to visual—contact. After all, I hadn't planned on having my visit to Burma cut short, and prematurely at that.

I could feel the blood pounding in my temples, a surge of adrenalin like a shot of methamphetamine. It gave me that needed edge, a burst of speed and self-confidence which saw me hit the last creaking stair and then the narrow basement corridor. Luckily enough, the storeroom door was still unlocked, though not for long. I slipped inside and slid the bolt into place.

Once again, it was impossible to see in front of me without resorting to my flash. I kept the beam low, directed at the dust-covered floor, then found a path through the assortment of uncatalogued and unrepaired artifacts. When I reached the window I stuck the flashlight back into my pocket, slipped Wilhelmina into her holster, and hoisted myself up to the edge of the sill.

Careful of the broken glass, I wiggled forward, twisting from left to right so that one shoulder and then the other could fit through the narrow opening. As soon as my arms had cleared the window, as soon as I felt the fresh air hit my cheeks, the rest was easy. I kept pulling myself forward until my hands were free, palms flat against the hard-packed dirt of the alleyway. Then, crawling on the ground like a soldier on maneuvers, I kept at it until my legs joined the rest of me and I'd seen the last of the window.

Quickly, I got to my feet, put the screen back into place and started down the alley in the direction of Phayre Street.

Once again, I didn't get very far.

An army Jeep, headlights piercing the darkness with a flood of glaring yellow light, was parked directly in front of the alley, barring my way. I stepped back, pressed myself flat against the wall of the building and moved cautiously in the opposite direction. I had no idea where I would end up. But there was no other choice, no other escape route, either.

It was all too apparent that Rangoon lacked a civilian police force. And it was just as apparent that the authorities weren't taking the break-in lightly. No doubt they feared an international episode, unpleasant repercussions, recriminations from the Chinese for failing to safeguard the priceless exhibit. But whatever the hell they were fearing, I was fearing it more. I didn't know how in God's name I was going to get back to the hotel, not when the Cultural Institute seemed to be crawling with soldiers.

To say that I was outnumbered would be putting it mildly. I kept backing away, hugging the wall, not stopping until I reached the opposite end of the garbage-strewn alleyway. The Ministry's headquarters now took a right-angle turn. But when I peered out to see if it was safe to make my move, one glance told me that safety was the last thing I'd find.

The rear of the building looked out onto a wide grassy lawn, one that was encircled by a high cyclone fence. It was a sculpture garden, dotted here and there with ancient statues of carved stone. Buddha looked back at me with a beneficent smile, silent and all-knowing. Behind him a three-headed elephant and a stylized lion, both symbols of war. The garden itself was brilliantly illuminated by a score of floodlights. On the other side of the fence there were at least half a dozen Jeeps, their headlights ablaze, focused my direction. Even as I watched, a detachment of troops, more than a dozen carbine-equipped soldiers, was sweeping across the manicured lawn like a plague of locusts.

I slipped back into the shadows and looked over my shoulder. The Jeep was still parked in front of the alley. Phayre Street was blocked. The building adjacent to the museum lacked a convenient row of basement windows. I had two choices, neither of them particularly appealing.

Either I try to make it across the garden and chance being mowed down by any one of a dozen soldiers, or else I work my way back towards Phayre Street and try to figure out a way to get past the Jeep.

I peered out once again. Twelve against one just wasn't fair, any way you slice it. I turned around and inched my way along the wall, moving closer and closer to the Jeep, to Phayre Street, to the escape that was so far eluding me. I could hear voices now, someone giving orders, barking out commands.

"You, over there, circle around the back," I translated to myself. Then I heard, "Don't just stand there. I want you men to make a sweep of the first floor. Perhaps he's still inside." And finally, "What about that storeroom? Are you positive he's still not hiding there? Did you go over it, inch by inch?"

What pissed me off more than anything else, more than the soldiers, the flood lamps, and the Jeep which blocked my escape route, was the fact that I still hadn't located the roll of microfilm. But I'd be of no use to AXE if I didn't make it back to the hotel, in one piece. I reached inside my pants and removed Pierre. The tiny gas bomb had served me once already, back in Hong Kong. Now, I hoped he'd prove as blinding and efficacious as the last time.

Well, the only way to find out was to try it. And that was precisely what I did.

With what I hoped was a well-aimed toss, I lobbed Pierre over the Jeep, right into the middle of Phayre Street. Someone gave a startled yell and then I was running. I kept my head down, saw the swirling choking cloud of Chemical Mace and darted around the side of the Jeep, right in front of its headlights. The staccato crack of a high-powered heavy caliber slug broke above the sound of retching, coughing voices. I didn't stop to look back, tearing down Phayre Street, though not in the direction I'd originally wanted to take. I had no idea where I was going, save for the fact that it was as far away from the Cultural Institute as my legs could carry me.

Another slug whistled overhead, nearly creasing my scalp. The lights were right on top of me and I zigzagged, left to right and back again, trying to elude the deadly gunfire. Behind me came the sound of running footsteps, at least three men already in pursuit. The one saving grace was that the gunfire stopped abruptly. Apparently, they couldn't get off a round without slowing down.

My breath was like fire, the dust of the alleyway rising up, nearly as choking as the gas which Pierre had so efficiently discharged. I kept looking for an alternate route, but so far there just wasn't any. The street consisted of wooden fences and building fronts, doors locked against intruders and intelligence agents.

"Hey you, stop or I shoot!" a voice cried out in the darkness, now that I'd managed to outdistance the glaring headlights. The words were spoken in Burmese, but I didn't need an interpreter. The soldier's tone of voice was warning enough.

Then I saw my opening and I took it without thinking twice, without a moment of hesitation.

It was nothing more than a path, twisting its way between two sagging wooden houses. I darted off Phayre Street and struggled to make out the details. I was afraid to use my flash, afraid to break my stride lest my pursuers catch up to me and nail me before I had a chance to make good my escape.

Suddenly I hit something, stumbled and lost my balance. I was still rolling as I heard a woman's high-pitched frightened voice, crying out in her native tongue. Apparently, I'd run right into the middle of an entire family, all camped out amidst the dirt and garbage. A baby howled fearfully as I spoke in sharp, quick tones, warning them to be quiet, promising to pay them well for their cooperation.

The mention of *kyats* did the trick. I grabbed for the nearest blanket and pulled it over me, even as I heard the distant voices of my three pursuers.

"He went down here," someone yelled. Then the clatter of footsteps drowned out the crying of the baby.

The beam of a flashlight pierced the darkness. I held my breath and remained motionless beneath the grimy blanket. A bedbug or a louse bit the back of my neck. I winced and strained to hear what the soldiers were saying. The baby was still crying, but now its mother pressed it to her breast. It suckled greedily as the soldiers drew near prowling about the compound.

"Who's there?" someone barked.

"What . . . ? Who are you?" the woman called out, her voice filled with panic. "We have no money."

"We don't want your money, lady," the soldier replied. "Did you see anyone just now?"

"No, we were asleep," her husband said, a tremor in his voice.

"Damn, we lost him."

"The captain's not going to like it."

"Screw the captain."

The voices receded. I stayed where I was until I could no longer hear the soldiers' departing footsteps. Then I peered out. The narrow path was once again deserted. *"Chay-zoo tin pah-day,"* I said, thanking them for their help.

They were too frightened to say a word.

I dug out my wallet and removed a hefty wad of paper *kyats*. The money would probably keep them in food for a good three weeks, if not longer. I pressed the bills into the woman's hand.

"Chay-zoo tin pah-day," she whispered, looking at me with wide and incredulous black eyes.

Then I got to my feet and started down the path. Hopefully, I'd hit a major cross street, get my bearings, and figure out how to get back to the Strand. It was just a matter of time.

CHAPTER EIGHT

DAY TWO—second day of seven allowed by the Burmese government.

I was sleeping the sleep of the dead when someone started knocking on the door. At first I thought the persistent tapping was part of my dream. But finally I raised my head off the pillow and opened a single groggy, rheumy eye.

"Josh? It's me, Kate," she called out from the other side of the door. "You up yet?"

"I am now," I muttered. "One sec." I threw my legs over the side of the bed, grabbed the nearest thing I could find—in this case a sweaty pair of shorts, stumbled into them and unlocked the door.

"I'm sorry," she said, not the least bit embarrassed by my lack of clothes. "I didn't mean to wake you up."

I ushered her inside and shut the door behind her. "'s all right," I mumbled. "Just give me a few minutes to clear my head."

"I didn't realize you had that much to drink last night," she said, her eyes following me as I made my way to the bathroom.

"Too much," I lied. At least she wasn't asking why I'd slipped out her room in the middle of the night. Good to my word, it took me all of five minutes to pull myself together. When I stepped out of the bathroom she was perched on the edge of the bed, as prim and proper as when we'd first met.

"You won't believe what I just heard from the porter," she said as I started to get dressed.

"What?"

"Someone tried to break into the National Museum last night."

"You serious?"

"That's what he told me. You were at the exhibit yesterday, weren't you?"

I nodded my head, trying to say as little as possible. "I'm into chinoiserie." No sooner did I get the words out when I realized how funny, peculiar, they must have sounded. But Kate didn't give any indication of either disbelief or amusement, taking my comment at face value.

"That's what I thought," she replied. "I mean, you had dinner with the curator and all. But I feel kind of cheated, even more than disappointed."

"I'm not following," I said, buttoning my shirt.

"Well, one reason I stopped in Rangoon was to see the Han artifacts . . ."

"So what's stopping you?" I was glad I'd had the foresight to put away Wilhelmina, as well as Hugo and a replacement Pierre. Now, I turned away from the mirror and eyed Kate curiously.

"What's stopping me?" she repeated. "I guess you're still half-asleep. Or maybe I didn't mention it."

"Mention what?" and in the same breath, so as not to appear too interested, asked, "Hungry?"

"Very." She got to her feet. "The awful thing is, the Chinese have decided to withdraw the exhibit and ship it back to Peking."

"Really? Why?" I asked, trying not to betray the feeling of alarm I experienced the moment she mentioned Peking.

"Joshua, you really are asleep."

I yawned, just to make that doubly obvious.

"Because of the break-in, that's why," she explained.

"That's too bad," I said, my voice revealing just the

slightest edge of disappointment. But behind my sleepy half-opened eyes, I was fully alert. If the exhibit was going to be sent back to China I'd have to work fast, faster than I wanted her to realize. I ushered her out of the room, locked the door behind me and headed towards the elevator at the end of the hall.

It wasn't until we were seated before two plates of thin and runny duck eggs—not one of my all-time breakfast favorites—that she told me she intended to leave Rangoon the next day. "It's time I got up to Pagan and really got started on my work," she said, toying with her eggs. Then she looked up and stared me right in the eye. "How about joining me for a few days, Josh? Think you can . . . put up with me?"

"Hell," I said, trying to laugh, "sure I can put up with you. In fact, there's nothing I'd like better. Trouble is, Kate, I just don't have the time."

"Oh." She sounded very disappointed.

"Honest to God. If I could, I would. Really."

"Well, can't say that I didn't try. I guess I'm just an amateur when it comes to seductions."

"Come on now, that has nothing to do with it. You know that as well as I do, so stop feeling so sorry for yourself. It doesn't become you." I signalled a passing waiter, signed the check and got to my feet. "I hate to eat and run, Kate, but . . ."

"Sure, you go on, do your thing." She gave a funny, little laugh and looked down at her plate, repeating the previous night's performance.

"I'll see you later then. Have a good day." Damn right business and pleasure doesn't mix, I thought to myself. It never has and it never will.

"Hello, Mr. Aung Nu? Mr. Morley here. I just heard . . . yes, what a disgrace. I hope nothing was stolen."

The curator's voice cracked on the other end of the

line. "Terrible," he kept repeating. "A most terrible, reprehensible business. Never before has such a thing happened. Not once in my memory. And what is worse, the Chinese are up in arms."

"I understand they intend to close down the exhibit," I replied, trying to sound as aggrieved as Aung Nu.

"Absolutely so," he said. "Even now the Chinese cultural attaché is supervising the work of crating up the artifacts. Fortunately nothing was taken but one of the cases was damaged. The thieves were apparently attempting to make off with the jade funerary armor—"

"Crafted for Princess Tou Wan?"

"Yes, that's the one. Horrifying." I could imagine his eyeglasses fogging up in dismay. "I've been up all night. Some say three men were responsible. Others say four."

"Four?" I repeated, barely able to keep my voice in check.

"Yes. A gang of thugs, no doubt. Social criminals, if you ask me."

So Mr. X was still on my trail, I thought. Even if I hadn't seen the mysterious and unknown third party from Peking, he'd obviously seen me. "Was anyone hurt?" I went on, curious to know what had happened to British accent.

"Hurt?" he said with rising inflection. "I see you have not heard all the details, Mr. Morley. No matter, they will be in this afternoon's paper, I am sure. Yes, one man was hurt. Killed by one of our guards. But the authorities have no idea as to his identity. A Westerner, but without papers. Customs is looking into the matter now."

I clucked my tongue. "And I was so hoping to take another look at the artifacts. Are you certain they won't change their minds, Mr. Aung Nu?"

"Yes, as certain as I possibly can be. As I said, they are crating the artifacts right now, right this very minute, in fact."

"And then they'll fly them out, no doubt."

"Yes," he said, "eventually."

"I'm sorry. I don't think I follow."

"Oh, it's all politics, Mr. Morley." He gave a loud and weary sigh. But at least he wasn't troubled by my curiosity. "The museum is in an uproar. Shambles everywhere. Broken windows. Bullet holes. Blood . . . but you see what the difficulty is? Perhaps you don't. There are no established air routes between China—Red China, that is—and Rangoon. Not since the riots. The Civil Aviation Administration of China only flies into our country via Kumming and Mandalay. So, as a result, tomorrow morning the entire exhibit is going to be put on a train which makes a scheduled stop at the old capital. From Mandalay, the artifacts will be transported to the airfield and then flown into Kumming."

"You must get some rest, Mr. Aung Nu. You sound . . . frightfully unnerved."

"Worse," he said. He attempted to chuckle and failed miserably. "But I suppose there is nothing to be done about it now. It's a . . . I'm afraid the expression eludes me, Mr. Morley."

"A *fait accompli*, Mr. Aung Nu. It's already a *fait accompli*."

There was much to be done, and very little time to do it.

With my three imcomparable assistants hidden beneath my clothes, I left my room as soon as I got off the phone. Outside the hotel I turned down several offers to change *kyats* on the black market, grabbed the first available three-wheeler, and told the driver to take me to the railway station, over near the Bogyoke outdoor market.

It took close to an hour to make all the necessary arrangements, Burmese bureaucracy tied up in endless knots of red tape, countless forms, and a critical shortage of carbon paper. Fortunately, there was only one train leaving for Mandalay, so I knew it had to be the same one which would be carrying the exhibit. The journey of 430 miles would take somewhere in the vicinity of twenty-six hours. At least I wouldn't be pressed for time, once we pulled out of Rangoon.

Certain that the roll of microfilm was still hidden somewhere on the jade death suit, I needed a second chance to examine Tou Wan's armor. I hadn't been able to make that kind of detailed search back at the museum. Now, I hoped to do a far more thorough job, not about to give up until I'd turned the suit and its case inside out . . . perhaps discovering the identity of Poy Chu and Wai Tsang's murderer, in the process. In any event, this would be my last opportunity to go over the artifact, because once the exhibit arrived in Mandalay, I'd be out of luck. Needless to say, I had no intention of returning to the States empty-handed.

There was only one other piece of business that had to be attended to, once I left the railway station. Convinced that British accent would be able to give me some much-needed answers, I was now determined to find him—before he found me. It wasn't all that impossible, either, unless of course the man was holed up somewhere inside the Soviet embassy. But until I checked out every hotel in Rangoon, I wouldn't be satisfied. Then and only then would I accept the possibility that he'd sought asylum inside the embassy compound. But not before.

Accordingly, I had my work cut out for me.

Despite the fact that Rangoon boasted a population of close to two million, there were only four hotels open to Western tourists. That narrowed my search down considerably. I crossed off the Strand, positive I would have already bumped into him had he registered there. Left with three choices, three possibilities, I walked over to the nearby YWCA hostel. It was open to both sexes and might just prove to be sufficiently anonymous and out-of-the-way to have attracted British accent and his sidekick.

The small and unprepossessing brick building was located on Bogale Bazaar Street, not far from the bustling outdoor market.

I told the desk clerk I was looking for two friends of mine—"A gentleman with a British accent and another man, heavyset, not very talkative."

He shuffled through a stack of index cards, each one bearing the name and passport number of the hostel's current guests. "Not here," he said. "Sorry," he added, as close-mouthed as the late KGB operative had been.

"Thanks."

Next stop was the Tamada, a short walk from the Shwe Dagon pagoda, Rangoon's most famous tourist attraction. Here, at the city's newest hotel, the clerk at the information desk proved to be an entirely different sort of customer.

"I cannot provide information," he said, pursing his lips.

"Why not?" I asked, trying my best to ignore his show of superciliousness. "They're old friends of mine and I understand they might be registered here."

"Is possible, certainly," he replied, glancing down at the register. He closed the ledger abruptly and looked beyond me, as though he'd already forgotten I was standing there, waiting for an answer.

"I know it's possible," I said. I tried to keep my voice down, my temper in check. "But I want to know if it's definite or not."

"I cannot give information." He adjusted the knot of his four-in-hand.

With a pained smile, knowing that a show of physical force would only get me thrown out by the burly and watchful doorman stationed across the lobby, I reached into my jacket pocket and pulled out my alligator billfold. I extracted a nice crisp 100 *kyat* note. It was worth about seven bucks American on the black market, considerably more at current government rates. The clerk took one look at the bill and pulled his lips back in an arrogant and affronted grin.

"You make joke," he said.

"I make offer," I replied.

"You have . . . razor blades, maybe?"

"What?" I said, not believing what I thought I'd heard.

"Blades for razor," he repeated, making the appropriate shaving gesture with his hand.

I shook my head. Either he was bananas or I was.

"Traveler's check then," he said promptly, nodding his head as though the negotiations were at an end.

I wrote out a ten-dollar traveler's check. "That should keep you in razor blades for the rest of the year," I said, passing it across the top of the counter.

Pleased with the transaction, he condescended to smile in my direction. "Now, you want to know about two men?"

"Yes," I said, and gave him a thumbnail sketch of British accent and his partner.

The clerk went through the register with a fine-toothed comb. When he looked up at me it was with an expression of disappointment. "Sorry," he said. "Not here."

"How about my traveler's check?"

"I no take bribe from tourists," he explained, and on this self-righteous note he turned his back on me and disappeared into his office.

Somehow, I just couldn't help but laugh.

Well, there was only one place left, way out on Kaba Aye Pagoda Road. The Inya Lake Hotel had been built with Russian aid a good ten years ago. According to what I'd read, it was first run by an Israeli firm, later taken over by the Burmese government tourist corporation. It overlooked the lake of the same name, a thirty-minute taxi ride from the center of the city.

Outside the Tamada, ten bucks poorer if a little bit wiser about what the guidebooks refer to as "the Burmese way," I bargained for a halfway decent rate with the driver of a waiting Jeep. The makeshift taxi—a "saloon Jeep" in local parlance—was considerably faster, and safer as well, than the three-wheeled jobs the city seemed to have no great lack of. I sat back in the seat, held onto the guard rail, and hoped the trip wouldn't be in vain.

The sun was already high in a cloudless and glaring blue sky. The streets were filled with the hurrying skirted figures of men and women. The swarms of gnats I'd seen and felt the previous evening had vanished with the mid-day sun. It was hot and sticky and my blazer did nothing to alleviate my discomfort. But without a jacket, there was no way I could conceal Wilhelmina from prying eyes and mischievous fingers. So I put up with the humidity and tried to relax.

It was easier said than done.

I was too hyped up, too anxious to find out if I was on a wild goose chase or if the ride out to the Inya Lake would prove to be well worth the time and trouble. It didn't surprise me when the driver asked for razor blades instead of a tip, once he pulled up under a cracking concrete marquee, a kind of awning cum canopy cum proof that the Russians just don't build things the way we do. The hotel was bleak, to put it mildly. The poured concrete had been left unfinished, replete with rust drippings, numerous fissures, and an air of general decay.

Not the kind of place British accent's probably used to, I thought to myself.

I paid the driver, gave him a genuine Federal Reserve Note in the sum of one dollar as a display of Western gratitude and appreciation, and sauntered into the bare and shabby lobby as nonchalantly as possible. The clerk at the front desk was a woman. It was a refreshing change, particularly since she was decked out in a mind-boggling, eye-opening, *longyi-ingyi* combo, which was just about as transparent as a length of Saran wrap.

"Good afternoon."

"Good afternoon, sir," she said. She made a point of ignoring my admiring stare. "May I help you?"

You sure can, I thought, though I managed to pull my eyes away, all the same. I stated my business as simply and succinctly as possible. I was already reaching for my wallet when she gave me the answer, the information I'd been hoping to hear all morning.

"Yes, your friends are staying here," she said with a smile, pleased to be of help. "They checked in two days ago. In fact, unless I am mistaken, Mr.," she said and stopped just long enough to examine the register. Fortunately, she didn't stop to examine me, or ask me to fill in the missing blank. "Your friend Mr. Carrington hasn't left his room all morning."

"That's Carrington, all right," I said with a grin. "Lazy bloke, bloody well always has been," I muttered, giving it my best stiff-upper-lip colonial swagger. "But what about his business associate?"

"Mr. Smith?"

"Yes." If Lithuania's answer to Lucky Luciano was named Smith, I might just as well start calling myself Ivan Popov.

She shook her head. "I do not like to keep—"

"Tabs."

"Yes, keep tabs, a check on our guests. He may still be sleeping, but I have not seen him since last evening. But I am sure your friend, Mr. Carrington, can tell you where he has gone."

That's for sure. "And that's room number . . .?"

"Six-o-nine." She pointed to the bank of elevators on the other side of the lobby.

"You've been most helpful," I said. "I'm very much obliged."

"Thank you." She smiled shyly. "Have you found your trip to Burma . . . interesting?"

"Extremely."

Well, one thing was certain. It was time to renew old acquaintances.

I took the elevator up to the sixth floor, got out, and walked cautiously down the hall. Wilhelmina was as ready as I was, smooth and hard and cool against my palm. When I reached 609, I stopped before the door and listened. There wasn't a sound coming from Carrington's room. I knocked softly, waited for a reply, then knocked a second time. Either he was sound asleep or else he was trying very hard to discourage visitors.

I had the square of acetate with me, but first I reached for the knob and jiggled it from left to right, one side to the other. The door swung open, which was very odd indeed. The floor-to-ceiling draperies were drawn across the windows. The room was shrouded in darkness, the air close and sweaty. I waited by the door, straining to hear a single telltale sound. Nothing came back but the creak of the floorboards beneath my feet. I held Wilhelmina at arm's length and took a single wary and stealthy step into the room. My eyes adjusted to the darkness and I could see the outline of a body beneath the sheets.

"Carrington, ole buddy," I called out in a hoarse whisper.

He didn't answer.

I whirled around, even as I slammed the door shut behind me. But there was no one waiting on the other side, anxious to catch me off my guard. All I saw was a bentwood chair, piled high with clothes and dirty laundry. I flicked on the overhead light and took another cautious step forward. "Carrington?" I said again. When he didn't answer I approached the bed and shook him. "Carrington!"

With my one free hand I grabbed hold of the edge of the bedcovers and pulled them back. Carrington was there all right. But he was in no shape to talk ... or do anything else.

CHAPTER NINE

Carrington looked up at the ceiling as though he were contemplating the lousy paint-job, the water stains, the flaking plaster. His eyes were wide and glassy, a dried-out blue that seemed to demand the decency of pennies. I didn't have any small change on me, so I lowered his lids with two fingers and hoped they'd stay that way. The first thing I thought was that he'd been caught off his guard, murdered the way Poy Chu and Wai Tsang had been killed, back in Hong Kong. But when I pulled the sheets down to the foot of the bed, one glance told me that my initial hypothesis didn't hold water.

A towel, once white and how dyed a clotted and uncommonly muddy shade of red, was pressed like a bloody compress to Carrington's side. I looked behind me and saw what I'd missed when I'd first entered the room: a faint but noticeable trail of blood from the door to the bed. No doubt the agent had taken a slug the night before back at the museum. He'd managed to escape and make it back to the hotel, only to crawl into bed and stay there. Permanently.

I pushed the blood-soaked towel aside and saw the bloody wound. The cartridge had shattered a rib and was probably still lodged inside his lung. If the external bleeding hadn't gotten him, the internal pulmonary hemorrhaging would have finished him off, sooner or later.

Well, there was nothing I could do for the guy, nothing the museum guards hadn't already taken care of.

I made sure to lock the door from the inside before starting my Sherlock Holmes routine, minus deerstalker and trusty Watson. The game was afoot, all right, taking off like gangbusters when I discovered a pile of ashes in the wastebasket under the bathroom sink. I sifted through them, came up with a thumbnail-sized scrap of charred paper of the kind used for passport covers. It must have belonged to the late Mr. Smith, because Carrington's passport was lying on top of the dresser.

Lloyd Carrington was carrying a Hong Kong passport, as meticulous a forgery as any I'd ever seen before. The leatherette cover was a shade too dark, but it would have taken only the most discerning and knowledgeable customs inspector to make that kind of determination.

Probably the work of Albinoni, I thought, remembering my unhappy dealings with the master Italian forger. Last I'd heard, he was living on a fat government pension, somewhere on the outskirts of Leningrad. Well, it was all too apparent that the Russians—the KGB, that is—were still getting their money's worth.

But the clincher, the one clue which confirmed all of my suspicions concerning Carrington's link with Moscow, was something I discovered when I examined the agent's automatic.

It was a Browning .380, short, compact, and about as deadly a weapon as they come. I put it on safety, released the magazine latch, and emptied it of ammunition. There was only one cartridge left out of a possible half-dozen. Ammunition the world over is given an identifying mark by its manufacturer, usually found etched around the primer in the middle of the cartridge base. The Browning's ammo wasn't the exception to the rule. But when I took a good close look at the high-caliber slug, it didn't bear anything as recognizable as Speer, Peters, or Norma, all American-based firms. Instead, I found myself relying on my knowledge of Russian, the Cyrillic alphabet in particular. The bullet had been manufactured in the Soviet

Union, even if the Browning itself had been assembled back in the States.

Soviet ammo just isn't sold on the open market, which told me nearly everything about Carrington I'd wanted to know but hadn't had the chance to ask.

Apparently, Poy Chu had sent out feelers to the KGB, just as I'd first suspected, hoping they would be interested in purchasing the spy list. I'm sure they were, judging from Carrington and Smith's presence at the museum the previous evening. Now, neither agent was in a position to buy anything, whether it be a roll of microfilm or a dispenser's worth of razor blades.

I pocketed the single remaining Soviet-made slug, as well as Carrington's phony passport. I figured it just might come in handy, particularly if I could manage to substitute my snapshot for his. Then I pulled the sheets over his head, found his white linen suit hanging in the closet, and laid it out at the foot of the bed. Hopefully, whoever discovered his body would get the message. After all, Carrington was obviously a clotheshorse. And the white linen suit would look a helluva lot more dapper than a shroud.

My competition was out of the running. But that didn't mean the rest of the mission would be smooth sailing. How could it be, when I was yet to meet up with my mysterious adversary, the person—or persons—responsible for two murders, and no doubt anxious to consummate a third, once I led them right to the microfilm. There was only one thing that bothered me, that didn't seem to fit neatly into place.

Aung Nu had said that four people had been seen at the museum, four "social criminals" as he called them. If number four was the agent from Peking, it was conceivable he had already examined the jade death suit while the exhibit was in the process of being packed and crated.

And if that was the case, he could very well be on his way back to China and I'd be out of luck. But that too was just another assumption to add to my fast-growing list. An alternate supposition was that party or parties unknown had arrived too late, had not seen either Carrington or myself at work on the suit. If that was what had happened, then they still didn't know where the microfilm was hidden. And I was still too valuable to be dispensed with, put out of operation, murdered as cold-bloodedly as Poy Chu.

But perhaps it wasn't even as complicated as all that. Perhaps they'd already secured the film. Perhaps they were now biding their time, anxious to finish the job by finishing off Nick Carter, Killmaster N3. With all the covers I'd assumed over the years, my identity still wasn't sacrosanct. As recently as a year before I'd been identified by a Chinese military advisor when I'd shown up in Katmandu. Peking intelligence would be more than happy—hell, they'd be delighted—to see the end of what they no doubt considered to be a long and all too successful career. The assassination of N3 would only make things easier for them in the future.

Not that any of these theories changed my plans. I still intended to board the Mandalay "express" the following morning, not about to give up or call it quits until I'd personally examined Tou Wan's funerary armor. If the microfilm wasn't there, well ... I'd have to deal with the problem when and if it occurred. But not before.

"I must be exceedingly dull company. You haven't said a word in ten minutes."

"Christ, I'm sorry, Kate. I guess I'm still a little hungover," I said. I looked across the table and smiled. She was right, though. I'd been sitting there, lost in speculation, trying to outguess my invisible opponent. Now, I turned my thoughts and my attention back to the blonde archaeology student who sat opposite me. "More wine?"

"Just a drop," she said. "And you haven't even touched your dinner."

"Their cooking leaves much to be desired."

"But you need to eat something to keep up your strength."

I laughed. "You sound like my mother."

"Then I won't say another word. If there's one thing I can't stand, it's being compared to someone's mother ... or sister, or high school sweetheart."

"If I didn't know you as well as I think I do, I'd say you were putting me on."

"I am," she said, and grinned and stuck out her tongue at me. "I guess I'll always be the girl next-door. Occupational hazard, I guess."

"There's nothing the matter with it, believe me," I assured her. "It's a time-honored role, as American as apple pie."

"Is everything satisfactory, sir?" the waiter asked, appearing alongside the table as if out of thin air.

"Perfect," I said. "Couldn't be better. Coffee, Kate?"

"Tea," she said.

"The lady'll have tea and I'll have coffee."

"Dessert?" he asked as he stacked the dishes.

"Kate?"

She shook her head.

"No, I don't think so. We Americans are very diet-conscious."

He smiled vaguely. As soon as he departed I looked back at Kate as I reached for a cigarette. "So ... here we are in Burma." I lit up and slouched back in my chair.

"Are you sure you haven't changed your mind?"

"About what?" I asked, letting my eyes linger on her face. Only the eyes were wrong, a bit too narrow and a bit too cool. But the rest of her was perfect. A straight, aquiline nose; full lips; all that cascading, shimmering blonde hair. I didn't want to give it up so quickly, even if I had no other choice.

"About going with me to Pagan," she explained.

The waiter reappeared and she lapsed into silence.

I took a sip of the strong black coffee, decided it was the best part of the undistinguished dinner, and set my cup down. "As a matter of fact, I've decided to go up to Mandalay, tomorrow morning."

"Mandalay?" Her eyes opened wide with interest, curiosity.

I nodded my head. "It's supposed to be a spectacular ride, lots of tropical scenery, local color, et cetera, et cetera," I said, trying to gloss over the fact that here I was leaving for Mandalay when I'd told her that morning my schedule didn't give me any time to accompany her to Pagan.

But my vacillating plans—fickle to say the least—didn't seem to bother her, or upset her one iota. On the contrary. "Well that's fantastic," she said. "You're taking the train that leaves tomorrow at ten-fifteen, aren't you?"

"Yes, but . . ."

"But that's the same train I'm going to be on." Judging from the expression on her face, she couldn't have been more delighted.

"No kidding." I tried to look pleased, but she'd really caught me by surprise. I hadn't counted on having a traveling companion, though there was nothing I could do about it now.

She nodded her head, as eager-eyed and energetic as a little kid. "You see, I take the Mandalay train for at least half of its run, a little more than that actually. I have to get off at—" She stopped in mid-sentence and tapped her fingers against the edge of the table. "Thazi . . . yes, that's the name of the town. It's about three hundred miles north of here. They told me at the railway station it should take anywhere between fifteen and eighteen hours to make the trip, so we'll really be able to . . . well, you know."

"You're blushing," I said.

"Am I?"

"You sure as hell are."

"Well ... I can't help it, Josh," she said, the color rising in her cheeks until her face was painted a uniform hot-pink.

"No, I guess not," I told her. "But it's very charming, Kate. A sign of—"

"Innocence?"

"You took the word right out of my mouth." I kept a smile in place as I led her from the dining room. But behind my grin was a frown which wouldn't go away. Suddenly everything was becoming much too complicated. Now, I had no choice but to include Kate in my plans, whether I liked it or not.

CHAPTER TEN

DAY THREE—third day of seven allowed by the Burmese government.

The scene at the railway station was pandemonium. Even before the train pulled in, the platform was jammed with Burmese, peasants and bureaucrats, white-collar workers and squalling babies. People were literally camped out alongside the tracks, waiting to get a seat. Customs didn't hassle us inspecting our bags, though an official disappeared with our passports and kept us waiting for a good thirty minutes. When he finally returned he just handed them back to us without a work of explanation. It wasn't worth getting into an argument about, or getting upset about.

By the time we passed through the gate to the platform, the train was finally moving slowly down the tracks. Both of us had reserved sleepers in the single Pullman car. The rest of the train, save for one car commandeered by the army, consisted of vintage coaches with row upon row of hard, slatted wooden benches and a rank and rancid smell of sweat and urine descending like a pall the moment the doors were opened.

"Maybe I should have taken a plane," Kate said as I helped her board the train.

"Well, it's too late now. Besides, this is the only way to get to see the countryside. Right?"

"Right," she said, though her voice didn't carry very much conviction.

Once I got her situated in her compartment I ducked out, ostensibly to buy some fruit from a vendor who was making his rounds up and down along the station platform. But I was really much more interested in cargo, not coconuts. I hotfooted it down the length of the platform until I came to the baggage car. The Han Dynasty artifacts were being loaded onto the train. The Chinese cultural attaché was supervising the work, while an armed detachment of Burmese soldiers stood guard nearby. I ducked out of sight, not wanting to be seen, particularly if Aung Nu had come down to the train station to see the collection off. Finding me on the same train as the exhibit would only be pushing coincidence to the breaking point. I didn't think the curator suspected that I had anything to do with the break-in and that's just the way I wanted things.

From where I stood I had a perfect view of the proceedings. The cultural attaché was the only Chinese national in attendance. Which meant that my mysterious adversary was either on the train or already on his way back to Peking. But wherever he was, I hoped to hell he hadn't located the microfilm.

I returned to the front of the train, bearing an armful of fresh fruit. "We'll never finish it all," Kate laughed when she saw what I'd brought back.

"Then we'll pass it out and have ourselves a party." I was trying my best to act like nothing was bothering me, particularly her company. I don't know how good a performance I was putting on, but Kate didn't seem to notice, didn't seem to act as if anything were amiss.

It was close to twelve when the train finally pulled out of the station. The delay was fine with me, because I had no intention of making my search until it got dark. The only difficulty was that Kate would be getting off the train sometime early the next morning. I'd have to conduct my examination while she was asleep. There was just no way to get around it.

She kept up a lively stream of conversation for the first hour or so, then lapsed into silence. I started to ask her about Pagan, but she begged off with a yawn and the announcement that she intended to take a nap. I glanced at my watch. It was 1:52. I had a long wait ahead of me, and whether it was going to be worth it or not was still up for grabs.

The train was the last thing from an express. All through the afternoon it made innumerable stops at innumerable little villages between Rangoon and Mandalay. Needless to say, there were just as many delays. Women ran up and down the various platforms, hawking their wares. Some had straw baskets strapped to their backs from which they dispensed any number of different varieties of tropical fruit: mangoes, rambutans, durian, and mangosteens. I made a point of sampling nearly every kind. What with the fruit I consumed along the way and the fruit I'd bought back in Rangoon, Kate looked at me as if I was losing my mind. I wasn't. There was a method to my madness. I had to think up a pretty sound excuse why I wouldn't be spending the night with her—our last night together, in fact. I figured that if I pleaded the worst case of upset stomach imaginable, I might just get away with it. Still, I drew the line when one of the women tried to interest me in a native delicacy I had neither the stomach nor the courage to sample. Five tiny birds—heads and legs still intact—were roasted to a crisp reddish-brown, then skewered on a stick she waved before our half-open window.

"Is good, is good," the woman kept repeating, first in English and then in Burmese. *"Ah lung kaung pa da."* She smacked her lips and patted her stomach, all for dramatic effect.

But I wasn't about to change my mind.

"What did she say?" Kate asked.

I was surprised Kate didn't speak Burmese, even if only a smattering of the language. After all, she was going to be living in Pagan for five weeks, working with the locals. "Very good," I finally translated.

"Yes, *hoke ket*," the woman agreed. "Ve-dy good."

"Go on, try it," Kate said with a laugh, goading me on.

"I'm sure they're wonderful," I told the woman as she continued to wave the skewer back and forth in front of the window. "But I'm full. I couldn't possibly."

She shrugged her shoulders and continued down the platform.

"You really should've tried it," Kate said, still playing the devil's advocate.

"And get even sicker than I already am?"

"Aren't you feeling well?"

I clutched my stomach and rolled my eyes around until she laughed. "Let's just say I've been known to feel better, and leave it at that."

There was a three-hour delay at the village of Nyaunglebin, a hundred miles north of Rangoon. I wanted to get off the train and go exploring, but there were all sorts of customs officials on the platform. No one was allowed to leave the station, so I had to content myself with stretching my legs. I took the opportunity to saunter down toward the rear of the train, curious to know if the delay had anything to do with the traveling exhibit. Six or seven Burmese soldiers squatted on their haunches, right alongside the baggage car. Their carbines were slung over their shoulders and they weren't paying much attention to their valuable freight. Still, there wasn't nearly enough time to make my search. I'd just have to bide my time and wait until dark.

I had to wait a little longer than that, actually.

It was nearing eleven that night when Kate finally got to her feet and asked me to help her set up her sleeper. I pulled the pallet-sized bed down from the wall, arranged the pile of linen the porter had given us and backed off toward the door. She was reaching for the zipper to her skirt when she stopped, her fingers frozen in place.

"Anything the matter, Josh?" she asked, her eyes registering a mixture of surprise and alarm.

"Everything."

"What?"

"I really feel sick. I don't think I'll be very good company tonight, Kate. I'm sorry." On that unhappy note I suddenly gagged, pressed one hand to my mouth and did an about-face. I fumbled for the latch on the sliding door, feigning—though not totally—the worst possible case of nausea. "Can't talk, can't talk," I muttered, letting it be known that if I didn't get out of the compartment, I couldn't be held responsible for the consequences.

"You poor baby," she said as she pulled the door open for me.

The poor baby fled down the center aisle, heading in the direction of the bathroom.

I holed up in the squalid little john—a hole in the floor and a cigar box worth of torn newsprint—for as long as my sense of smell could stand it. Then I slipped into my compartment and dug through my toilet kit until I found the ten milligram tabs of prochlorperazine I'd made sure to take along. The anti-emetic would keep the fruit down, combating the nausea as well. I made up my bed, gave Wilhelmina a thorough cleaning, and stretched out on the paper-thin mattress.

Gradually, the gastrointestinal discomfort subsided. The train lulled me into a semi-somnolent state. I waited until the other passengers were all bedded down for the night before I finally got to my feet and slid the compartmen door open. My Rolex glowed 12:17. I eased the door shut behind me and started down the center aisle, passing from the Pullman into the adjoining car.

The straight-backed wooden benches were crammed to the gills with Burmese and their baggage. Even with the windows open, the air was close and tight. A group of travelers played cards in a corner. As I headed down the aisle, they stopped just long enough to watch me, silent and curious. I gave them my best un-Ugly American smile and kept walking. The next three cars were a repetition of the first, filled to capacity. People were even stretched out on the floor, their meager belongings piled all around them. I stepped carefully, now, not particularly anxious to come down on someone's head or fingers. A colicky baby cried fitfully. Someone hummed a tune that sounded vaguely familiar, while on the other side of the dusty and unwashed windows the Burmese night paraded by in all its blue-black glory.

Funny kind of situation, isn't it, Nick, I thought to myself. Here are all these people, eking out some sort of life for themselves, and here you are, playing super-spy.

Only difference, I wasn't really playing. Everything was for keeps. And everything centered upon recovering the microfilm. I glanced back. The car was filled with shadows. Someone snored softly in his sleep. Another baby gave a whimper and fell silent. No one was following me, neither Mr. X, Y, or Z.

Two more creaking cars later, I was standing before the baggage compartment. I took a deep breath, tasted the night air, and reached for the recessed handhold to open the door. The heavy metal door groaned loudly as I slid it back along its track. Three dazed, sleepy faces instantly looked up at me, none too friendly, either.

"No allowing," one of the soldiers said, motioning me back, even as I stepped into the car and eased the door shut behind me.

"What?" I said in English.

All three men got warily to their feet. "No allowing," a second guard repeated.

The third soldier nodded his head in agreement. "Not ... permitted," he said, struggling to get the word out.

Behind them I could see the piled crates with their Chinese ideograms, all the Han Dynasty artifacts labeled and carefully packed to insure against breakage. One of the soldiers, his carbine bouncing along his back, started toward me. I broke into Burmese, which had an immediate calmative effect. I even got one of the men to smile.

"Everyone's asleep," I said. I motioned behind me, as though referring to the entire trainload of passengers. "I've been looking for someone to share a cigarette with. Care to join me?" I asked as I reached inside my jacket and pulled out my gold cigarette case. I snapped it open and extended it before me.

"Thank you," one soldier after another replied as each reached for a smoke.

I had my Dunhill in readiness. The flame wavered before their boyish and unsuspecting faces. A single safety lamp glowed softly behind us as I squatted down and rested on my heels and the back of my legs, waiting for them to join me. Slowly they crouched down, commenting on the excellence of the tobacco.

"I'm a reporter for a magazine in Great Britain," I went on, wondering what kind of accent an Englishman would use when speaking Burmese.

"A writer?"

"Yes. I've been doing an article about the Chinese exhibit," I said, motioning directly behind them to the collection of wooden crates, one of which contained Tou Wan's jade death suit. "Lloyd Carrington." I extended my hand by way of introduction.

"You stay in Burma, Rangoon?" one of the young men asked, obviously quite proud of his knowledge of English.

I nodded my head. "At the Inya Lake Hotel."

"Not so good as Strand," he replied with a laugh and a flash of evenly spaced white teeth.

"The Strand was too expensive," I said, grinning goodnaturedly. Very slowly, careful of sudden moves, I got back to my feet and leaned against the nearest crate. I blew a smoke ring into the air and kept up the conversation, though it was fast becoming apparent that the three guards had other things on their mind, namely sleep. Even as I continued to talk to them, barely aware of what I was saying, I was moving in the direction of the rear of the baggage car, closer and closer to the packing crates. Idly, I tapped my fingers against the first wooden box I came in contact with.

"We must ask you to return to your compartment," one of the soldiers announced. He straightened up and tamped out his cigarette with two fingers before putting the rest of the stub away in his pocket.

"Why?" I said in English, my fingers sliding toward my shoulder holster.

"Is not allowed. Not permitting," he said. He stepped toward me and I held my ground, waiting for him to move even closer.

"Come, Mr. Carrington. We will get into trouble," he said, reverting back to his mother tongue.

I ground out my cigarette beneath my heel. "I just want to show you something," I said.

"What?"

"Something that'll make you laugh," I explained. "Come here a sec. It's . . . how do you say?" I said, making a universally understood obscene gesture with my hand.

He broke into a toothy grin and stepped toward me. I slid my hand under my jacket and pulled Wilhelmina out of retirement and the Luger's blued finish blazed up before his wide and astonished eyes.

"I . . . I not understand," he stammered in disbelief.

"It's really quite simple, my friend." I had Wilhelmina at his neck and his M-14 off his shoulder before he even realized what was happening. Then with my free hand I pulled him around, shielding myself with his trembling body. The two other soldiers had already gotten to their feet. Before either of them could make a move or cry out a warning, I spoke quickly. "One move, one sound, and your friend here will be on his way to Nirvana. Is that clear?"

"Hoke ket," they whispered. "Yes."

"Very good. Now lower your weapons to the floor. That's it, nice and easy. No one's going to get hurt, as long as you cooperate." I pressed Wilhelmina flush against the soldier's neck, a half nelson keeping him immobilized. When the carbines had been lowered to the floor I let go of my prisoner and shoved him forward. I reached inside my blazer and hauled out the length of nylon rope I'd made sure to take along. "Remember," I warned him, "if you do exactly as I ask, no one's going to get their heads blown off. Understood?"

"Hoke ket," whispered three separate voices, one right after another.

"Excellent," I tossed the soldier the length of coiled rope, instructing him to tie up his two friends, securing their ankles together and then roping their hands behind their back.

Afraid of Wilhelmina's hair trigger, the young Burmese soldier did precisely as I had ordered. As for his two army buddies, they were just as cooperative, just as frightened. The truth of the matter was I didn't want to use Wilhelmina, not if I could help it. I had a silencer in my pocket, ready to attach to the Luger should events dictate that kind of rash action. But I hoped it wouldn't come to that. They were kids. They probably didn't even know the significance or value of what they were guarding.

The soldier worked quickly, the sight of Wilhelmina all the inducement he needed. When his two friends were tied up, I told him to crouch down alongside of them. Experience, practice, had taught me just how efficacious the butt of a revolver can be. I brought it down against the back of the soldier's head with just enough power behind my swing to knock him cold without giving him a concussion. The sharp rap of metal against bone caused his two fellow soldiers to stiffen with fear, even as their friend crumpled to the floor.

"He'll have a splitting headache when he wakes up," I told them, "but that's about all." I'd already prepared separate lengths of torn linen which I now put to use, gagging each soldier in turn. I checked their bonds, made sure the knots were tied securely, and then locked the sliding door from the inside. "Just stay put and everything'll be fine."

I glanced at my wrist. The Rolex read 12:51. Everything was going according to schedule. I turned away from my three captives and looked for the familiar ideograms which would read Tou Wan. The coffin-sized crate, precisely the dimensions I'd expected it to be, was located at the extreme rear of the baggage car. I moved various crates aside until I could get to it. When I glanced back, the two soldiers who were bound and gagged were following me with wide and terrified eyes. I was glad they valued their lives. It made things a lot easier for all concerned.

"It'll be all over before you realize it, guys," I said, removing a miniaturized set of tools from my jacket pocket. It seemed to take forever before I managed to pry off the lid of the wooden case. I set it down alongside me and dug through the excelsior until my eyes were rewarded with the sight of blue-green jade, fine lines of gold wire criss-crossing the over two thousand individual stone plaques.

The seconds kept ticking by as I hurried to remove the cumbersome glass cover of the museum case. I was afraid that any minute someone would try to enter the baggage car—their commanding officer, perhaps—only to discover that the door was locked from the inside. There was a crowded coach filled with soldiers on the other side of the freight compartment. I didn't want to bring any of them on the run, even if they had to climb over the top of the baggage car in order to reach the door. So I worked even more quickly than before, trying to get a good grip on the lip of the glass cover.

One of the soldiers started to groan behind his gag. I swiveled around, aligned the bead of Wilhelmina's sights on the man's head, and waited for him to get the message. A single glistening tear dripped down his cheek. He nodded his head at me, as if to say "It won't happen again," and lowered his eyes. I turned back to the problem at hand.

Ten minutes later I had the lid off. I set it carefully aside and reached not for the suit itself, but for the maroon felt backing on which it was laid out. Strips of cloth had been secured around the death suit and the sides of the wooden case, so as to prevent the armor from rattling around while it was in transit. I cut through them with the blade of my pocketknife and peeled off the felt liner. I had to ease the suit to one side in order to completely remove the cloth covering.

But even after I'd exposed the entire unfinished wood surface of the case, the roll of microfilm was nowhere to be found. I looked back at my captives. They were still watching me, silent and unmoving.

It has to be here, I kept telling myself, unwilling to give up, call it quits, concede defeat. Come on, Carter. Use your imagination. Where could he have hidden it? He was one of the best double-agents in the business. Cleverness was his middle name. But God knows that's never been one of your shortcomings, either. So think. Think.

It wasn't under the felt.

It wasn't under the suit.

I'd already examined the *huangs* and *pi*, and the film wasn't there either.

Where else?

I raised the head of the funerary armor and grabbed hold of Tou Wan's pillow. The gilded and jade-inlaid bronze headrest was surprisingly light. A solid chunk of bronze would have felt pretty hefty. But the sculpted and ornately decorated metal wasn't heavy at all.

It's hollow, I realized. Which means that—

I didn't stop to ask myself anymore questions.

Working my fingers across the surface of the artifact, I searched for a loose plaque, some sort of device— mechanical or otherwise—which would reveal the interior of the object. A hollow headrest meant that Poy Chu, or someone in his employ back at the Peking Museum, had substituted the real bronze pillow for a skillful imitation. As ornate and fancifully decorated as the object happened to be, it was as patently phony as a three-dollar bill. I struck it against the side of the wooden packing case. One corner broke off like the chipped and flaking ceiling in Carrington's hotel room. It wasn't bronze and it wasn't even jade, just artfully and cleverly painted plaster of Paris—*trompe l'oeil* at its very best.

The two guards looked at me with horror-stricken eyes, finding it inconceivable that I was "vandalizing" the precious art treasure. It was precious all right, but for altogether different reasons. I struck it sharply once again. The plaster headrest cracked neatly in two. And there it was, wrapped in rice paper, the sole reason why I had traveled halfway around the world.

I was one step—one very significant step—ahead of Mr. X, wherever he might happen to be.

Quickly now, for it was already past one A.M., I unscrewed the back of my Rolex and deposited the roll of film right inside. There was room to spare. The watch was waterproof, anti-magnetic, you name it. The film would be perfectly safe until such time as I was at liberty to remove it from the stainless steel case.

But I still wasn't done.

1:21 read the Rolex's phosphorescent numerals as I began to work my way backwards, doing everything in reverse. First, I rearranged the felt backing, then slid the armor into place and tied the torn strips of cloth together to prevent the burial suit from sliding around inside its case. Next, I lowered the bulky glass cover and then piled on all the excelsior I had removed a few minutes earlier. Finally, I replaced the top of the packing crate and nailed it securely into position. I buried two broken halves of the specious headrest under a pile of crates, knowing it would take quite awhile for them to be discovered.

1:35. Unless I'd miscalculated, we wouldn't be pulling into the station at Thazi for a good five hours. There was still some rope left and I put it to use, securing the unconscious soldier's hands behind his back, then making sure his ankles were pinioned tightly together. When he came to, probably within the next hour, he wouldn't be in any shape to move, to call for help. He was already gagged and I took the opportunity to make sure the other two guards hadn't loosened their bonds.

They hadn't.

Everything was taken care of, save for one last bit of business. I turned my back on the two watchful soldiers and removed Carrington's passport from my pocket. I let it slip from my fingers even as I turned toward the door. I could see one of the young Burmese fix his eyes on it. I wanted him to think the loss was accidental, as if I'd inadvertently left behind a highly valuable clue.

I released the locked bolt and looked back at the trussed up guards. "Try to get some sleep, fellers. It's gonna be a long night." I started to slide the door back. *"Thwah pah taw may,"* I called out. "Good-bye."

Carefully now, slowly, I eased the heavy metal door back along its track. A pair of wide and incredulous baby-blues returned my unblinking stare. The eyes focused over my shoulder, caught sight of the three guards who were all tied up in knots, and opened even wider. I slammed the door shut behind me and reached out, grabbing hold of her before she could run.

Kate Holmes looked as if she'd just seen a ghost.

CHAPTER ELEVEN

"What the hell are you doing here?" I hissed, trying to keep my voice down.

"What the ... me? You're asking *me*?" She tried to pull away but I held onto her arm with a viselike grip, not about to let her run off.

"Now listen to me," I said. I cupped her chin in one hand so that she was forced to acknowledge everything I said. "You're going to do just what I tell you to, is that clear?"

"No it is not clear," she said, defiant, too independent for her own good.

Before I had it out with her I dipped my hand into one of my trouser pockets and pulled out a small Yale lock I hadn't forgotten to bring along. I secured it to the outside of the sliding door. Every delay would count in my favor. Getting the lock off would take five or ten minutes— minutes I could very well put to use, making good my escape. When that last piece of necessary business had been taken care of, I pulled her away from the door until we were standing between the baggage car and the adjacent coach. The rickety iron floor shook and vibrated beneath our feet. The night winds whipped at her face, her blond hair flying in all directions. She kept brushing it back with one hand, still struggling to pull free.

But I wasn't ready to let go, to relinquish my grip. "You followed me," I told her. "I want to know why."

"Followed you?" she exclaimed. She sounded

breathless, but less frightened than she'd been a moment before. "I did no such thing!"

"Don't give me any of that crap," I snapped back. "Why the hell are you standing here, if you didn't follow me."

"I don't like it when you talk to me like that," she replied, reverting to her old role of Miss Goody Two-Shoes. Her voice cracked and her blue eyes turned milky, watery.

I looked behind her. No one was moving through the crowded car, heading in our direction. "I want to know why you followed me," I said again.

And again she insisted she hadn't done anything of the kind. "I was worried about you when you ... when you got sick," she stammered. "I couldn't sleep. The mosquitoes were driving me crazy. So I went to your compartment and when I found it empty it ... it made me nervous. I didn't know what to think. This is a very strange country, you know that."

"It's getting stranger by the minute," I said, more for my own benefit than Kate's. I still held onto her hand, but now I led her back through the darkened cars. The more distance I put between myself and the baggage compartment, the happier I'd be.

"You haven't told me what you were doing in there," she said.

"Just keep your mouth shut, Kate," I whispered. "Unless of course you want to get us both killed."

"Killed?"

"Damn right, sweetheart. I'm not playing games. This is for keeps, so just do exactly what I tell you to, okay? Believe me, the last thing I want is for you to get hurt."

She kept quiet after that, not saying a word until the two of us were back inside her sleeping compartment. I locked the door behind us and took a deep and weary breath. Whether I'd earned it or not was still up for grabs.

"You stole something from the exhibit, didn't you?" she said. She sounded wounded and aggrieved. "That's why you changed your mind at the last minute, isn't it?"

"Changed my mind about what?"

"About going to Mandalay. Instead of leaving Burma the way you said you were." Her hands flew up to her face, as though covering unseen scars, unshed tears. "Christ, I don't know what to believe anymore. I thought . . . I thought you were—"

"What?" I snapped back, barely able to keep my temper in check. "First of all, how the hell did you know the exhibit was going to be on this train?"

"I'm . . . I'm not stupid," she said. "It was in this morning's paper, for your information."

"And for your information, you don't read Burmese."

"They have an English-language column on page two. So don't accuse me of being a liar. That's one thing I'm not," she was quick to reply. "What is this, anyway? What kind of third-degree are you giving me? I didn't do anything wrong. You did. You're the guilty party around here, not me. You're the one who's the thief."

"I'm not a thief, Kate. I didn't steal anything from the exhibit that didn't belong to—" I stopped short. The less said, the better, I thought to myself. So I tried another approach, a different tack, anxious to convince her of my innocence without exposing anything that had to do with AXE. "Does it look like I'm carrying a Han artifact on me?" I went on. "Well, does it? Where the hell would I be hiding a 2000-year-old bowl, a figurine? Maybe you think I just shoved it up my—".

I stopped abruptly, and not because of her virgin ears, either. I held my breath, then raised a finger to my lips. On the other side of the locked door I could hear the sound of running feet; loud, anxious voices. Sonuvabitch, I thought. It didn't take them very long to figure out what happened. Now what?

Even though I'd left the passport behind to confuse the authorities, I realized it probably wouldn't do very much good. Once the guards were shown the snapshot on the inside cover, they'd know that Carrington and I were certainly not one and the same. The passport photo had been die-cut, stamped with a government seal which was impossible to duplicate. If I'd had more time I might have been able to find someone in Rangoon willing to do the work, forging that kind of raised seal on my own snapshot. Unfortunately, time was the one commodity I'd been in short supply of all along.

Right now they were probably looking for someone who fit my description. And there wasn't anyone else on the train who filled the bill the way I did.

There was an angry knock on the door. I looked frantically at Kate. She was my only hope. Without her help and cooperation it would be all over before I could do anything about it.

"*Hey, hey!*" someone called out. "Hello, Miss ... Holmes? Opening please. This are porter here."

Once again I turned my eyes in her direction, trying—if only by the expression on my face—to convince her of my innocence.

"What?" she said, sounding dazed, groggy with sleep. Hurriedly she began to pull off her skirt and blouse, replacing them with a rumpled terrycloth bathrobe.

"Is customs person and porter here," a second voice announced. The inspector rapped his knuckles against the door, demanding to be admitted to the compartment.

"One second, please. I was sleeping." She looked back at me and I nodded my head, scrambled under the sleeping ledge and flattened myself down against the floor. If they intended to search the compartment, there was no way they wouldn't find me. But I'd have to take that chance. I didn't have any other choice.

Kate switched off the light so that the cabin was suddenly filled with shadows, including my own. I held my breath and waited as she fumbled with the latch, finally unlocking the door. She slid it open a mere inch or so, as though protecting her modesty from the impertinence of prying eyes and midnight visitors. "Yes? What is it?" she asked, followed by one of the most convincing yawns I'd ever heard.

"We wishing to examine compartment," the customs inspector said, loud and authoritative, the kind of voice you just knew never accepted no for an answer.

"Whatever for?" She gave a shy and girlish laugh. "First you wake me up from a sound sleep and now you want to go through my belongings. I don't understand. I went through customs back in Rangoon, gentlemen."

"Excusing the . . . inconvenience," the official said. "But the porter saying you were with British gentlemen all afternoon. Is true?"

"You mean Mr. . . . Fitzhugh, I presume," she said, missing a beat. "Yes, as a matter of fact I was. Funny that you should ask."

"Why funny?" the porter said. He sounded confused and unsure of himself, no doubt unaccustomed to awakening young American women in the middle of the night.

"Why?" she repeated. "Because he was a very strange man. I thought he was odd . . . moody. But he got off at . . . what was that village after Nyaunglebin?"

"Toungoo?"

"Yes," she said with another persuasive yawn. "That must have been the place. He got off the train. I even waved good-bye. What about him, anyway?"

"He did not get off train, Miss Holmes," the customs officer replied, brisk and to the point.

"He didn't?" I could imagine the way she must have been batting her eyelashes, trying to convince them of her sincerity. "But of course he did, gentlemen. I saw him with my own two eyes. He waved good-bye and then . . . then he was gone."

"*Ma hoke boo*. I mean to saying—no," the porter corrected. "But you not seeing this . . . this man after Toungoo?"

"No."

"Ve-dy strange," he said. "Because this man breaking into baggage car, hurting soldier persons, stealing from valuable collection Chinese art work. Is ve-dy embarrassing for Burmese peoples, such thing to happening."

"It certainly is," she agreed.

"And now," the customs officer added, "he must be finding."

"Why that's terrible," she replied, clucking her tongue loudly. "Am I to understand this man I was with actually stole something that didn't belong to him? What are you going to do to find him? I hope he isn't armed, gentlemen. I thought Burma was a safe country, not like . . . those other places in Asia." Her baby-blues must have been going a mile a minute. I couldn't have been more pleased . . . or proud.

"Burma ve-dy safe," the porter assured her. "No worrying. We have soldier persons in all cars now. You ve-dy safe, I promising."

"And you still haven't found him, even with all your soldiers?" she exclaimed.

"Not yet," the inspector replied. "But soon we finding him. Next stop is Thazi. We put up barricades all along route between Thazi and Mandalay. But now we asking to look in your compartment, Miss Holmes."

"Why certainly," she said. "But I still don't see the point. I've been sound asleep for the last few hours."

A rectangle of soft amber light spilled across the threshold as she opened the door for them and stepped to the side. I could see two pairs of rubber-soled canvas shoes, two pairs of blue serge trousers. I edged back, pressing myself down into the narrow space below the sleeping platform. The feet stopped inches away from me and I heard the railway officials pulling back the curtains which concealed the bed. Kate's luggage was piled high in front of me, her skirt and blouse as well. If they bent down to examine her baggage, I'd be done for.

"What is that?" I heard the customs official ask.

"My bags," she said. "Which reminds me ... I almost forgot."

To tell them I was here? To what? I edged back as far as possible and reached inside my pants for Pierre. If I detonated the gas bomb and sprayed them all with Chemical Mace, they'd be rolling around the floor, writhing in agony as a result of the nerve gas. But I might just be writhing with them, unless I could get out of the compartment before they did.

I heard her bare feet—she'd kicked off her shoes moments before opening the door—hurrying toward me, then saw a pair of slim, white hands take hold of one of her bags. She undid the clasp and raised the lid. It was like a screen, one which only served to increase my chances, further concealing my presence below the sleeping ledge.

"I have some American cigarettes with me," she said in her gayest and most frivolous tone of voice. "I thought you might like to try them."

"American tobacco?" the porter said greedily. "You have maybe too ... a razor blade, Miss Holmes?"

It was an all too familiar refrain. But apparently she still believed in shaving her legs, because a minute or two later she was ushering both men out of the compartment, one razor blade and one pack of cigarettes for each. "And you're sure I'm safe here?" she said loudly.

"Ve-dy safe, ve-dy safe," the porter said, reassuring her once again. "No things to fear, Miss Holmes. And *chayzoo tin pah-day.*"

"Yes, thanking you," the customs inspector seconded. "*Chay-zoo tin pah-day.*"

"*Chay-zoo tin pah-day* to you," she said. The door slid shut behind her.

I waited behind the pile of suitcases until I could no longer hear the departing footfalls of the two officials. Only then did I scramble out of hiding and get quickly to my feet. Kate edged back until she was leaning against the far wall of the compartment. She looked at me as if I were a complete and total stranger.

"I don't know who you are," she said, her voice pitched so low it was hard to hear her. "But now you've made me your accessory . . . that's the expression, isn't it? An accessory after the fact? Well, what's the difference what it's called. It's done, whether I like it or not."

It would have made things a helluva lot easier for me if I could have told her she was merely doing her patriotic duty, if I could have explained what I'd found inside Tou Wan's phony headrest. But that kind of no-holds-barred honesty was out of the question.

"Thanks," I said, because that was about as much as I could say, under the circumstances. "I thought it was all over for a minute there. But you knew just how to distract them."

"Yes, I'm a very clever young woman, very resourceful. A real pro," she said with a laugh, one that was nine parts scorn and one part self-reproach. "And now what are you going to do, Josh? You'll never be able to get off the train without being recognized, apprehended. You heard what they said. They have soldiers in every car. Thazi's going to be a madhouse, what with police and soldiers and customs officials."

You're telling me, I thought to myself. I turned my eyes away from her and glanced at the dusty window above her bed. Dark shadows flew past, vaguely seen shapes of midnight-green set against a field of starless sky. The train lurched and rattled all around us and the night had a texture that was neither comforting nor supportive. There wasn't anything to hold onto, to grab for and cling tight. Accessory after the fact, I repeated to myself. She's right, too, whether I like it or not. I didn't want her around because I was afraid something like this might happen. And now it has and I can't do anything about it, either. It's too late for that, much too late.

"I want to say it one more time, Kate," I began, choosing my words with the utmost of care.

"Say what?" she asked, petulant, resentful. She wrapped her robe tightly around her, though the gesture had little if anything to do with the fact that she might be cold.

"Believe me, there's an explanation for everything. I didn't steal anything that was part of the exhibit, anything that belonged to . . . the Hans. Everything that was back in the museum in Rangoon is still in the baggage car. Everything."

"Then what *did* happen back there?" she asked, determined to get the explanation she obviously felt she deserved. "What were you doing in the baggage car, to begin with? And why were those soldiers tied up, bound and gagged?"

"If I could tell you, I would. You've just got to trust me, Kate, that's all I can say."

"Well I've done that already, haven't I?" It was a rhetorical question, one which didn't require a response. She laughed weakly, trying to dispel the gathering tension, the atmosphere of gloom and pessimism I could feel settling like ashes all around us. "So I guess there's no reason to stop now." She sighed deeply and made another concerted effort to brighten up. "What do you want me to do, Josh? I'm in this up to my neck, as it is. I might as well finish what I started."

I asked her what she had intended to do once she arrived in Thazi.

"I was supposed to switch trains and go as far as . . . Meiktila. From there I figured I'd hire a car to take me the rest of the way. I think Pagan's two or three hours drive, about fifty miles or so over back roads."

All the roads in Burma are back roads, cow paths, I thought with a frown. Even the famous road to Mandalay isn't a road at all. It's the Irrawaddy River.

I leaned back against the edge of the bed and tried to

think things through, logically and carefully. There would be no room for error, no place for a mistake. When I looked back at her her eyes were half-closed. She seemed exhausted, on the verge of collapse.

"Why don't you get into bed," I suggested. "Get some sleep . . . while you can."

"But what are you going to do? How are you going to get out of this?"

"It's all up to you," I finally admitted. Then I explained the plan I'd worked out, taking it slowly, one step at a time. She listened carefully, even as she climbed up onto the ledge and stretched out on the wafer-thin mattress. "Can you do it?" I asked after I told her what I had in mind.

She nodded her head. "I think so. But are you sure you won't get hurt?"

"That remains to be seen." I glanced at my watch. It was already 2:39. Some three hours to go, I thought. I crawled under the sleeper and pulled the luggage back into place, just in case the inspector and his assistant planned a return visit.

"Good-night," Kate whispered in the darkness. "Sleep tight . . . sweet dreams."

I laughed bitterly to myself and closed my eyes.

CHAPTER TWELVE

DAY FOUR—fourth day of seven allowed by the Burmese government.

Sleep came fitfully, if at all.

The rumbling of the Mandalay express echoed the rumbling of my stomach. I opened my eyes, saw that the compartment was filled with light, and looked hurriedly at my watch. It was a little after five-thirty, which meant that we'd reach Thazi in less than half an hour. I crawled out, got to my feet, and stretched my cramped muscles. Kate's eyes were closed, the fingers of one hand drawn up to her lips. I reached up and shook her gently. Her eyes opened wide the instant I touched her.

"Mornin'," I whispered.

"Good morning." She yawned and raised her arms above her head. "What time is it?"

"Five-thirty. Listen, I have to get my suitcase from the other compartment ... unless of course they've gotten it for me. As soon as I get back, I want you to go out into the corridor and ask the porter when we're expected in Thazi. Okay?"

She nodded her head. "Fine. I'll start getting dressed right away."

I headed toward the door.

Her voice reached out to me. "Be careful."

"That's my middle name." I eased the sliding door back and stuck my head out. Despite what the porter had told her, the passage was empty, neither soldiers nor carbines in evidence. I stepped out of hiding and tiptoed down the deserted corridor, not about to stop until I reached my compartment.

I pulled the door back, took one look, and lashed out with a flying kick, my entire thrust and weight centered on my rigidly held instep. The M-14 flew from the soldiers's hands and clattered loudly to the floor. He gave a startled cry and bent forward, trying to retrieve his weapon.

You shouldn't have done that, I thought.

The instant he bent forward, scrambling for the carbine, I sent my knee crashing into his side. I must have bruised the hell out of his kidney because he toppled over and inched back on his hands and knees, unable to get to his feet. A knife-hand slash to his ribs, followed by a swiftly executed *pan-de ji-lu-ki* or reverse punch to the guy's throat and he fell against the edge of the sleeping platform. His face was an ugly purple, his hands wrapped tightly around his chest. Even as he clutched at himself he was gagging, unable to breathe. A thin trickle of vomit, a bilious shade of green, erupted out of the corner of his mouth. But I wasn't finished with him. He'd obviously been sent here to wait for me and since he'd been on duty half the night, I wanted to give him something to really remember me by, something he wouldn't easily forget.

With a snap that was all instinct, I sent the toe of my shoe crashing into his forehead. Had I aimed for his larynx, his bobbing and vulnerable adam's apple, his family would have been hit with a bill for funeral expenses. But there was no reason to murder the kid. I just wanted to shake him up a little and then make sure he got the rest he deserved.

The guard's head flew back at a crooked and anatomically unfamiliar angle. He was out cold, and probably would remain that way for the rest of the morning, if not the entire afternoon.

I grabbed hold of my luggage and left as silently as I

had entered. I was back inside Kate's compartment before anyone else got wise to what had happened. Luckily, there wasn't anything very incriminating inside my suitcase. It was equipped with a false bottom. Judging from its weight, I knew it hadn't been tampered with.

"You're all out of breath," Kate said as I made sure to lock the door.

"I always like a little workout before breakfast. Keeps me on my toes."

She didn't know if I was serious or not. I didn't know, either.

"I'll go speak to the porter."

"I'll try to keep myself busy," and I gave myself the luxury of a laugh.

It fell on deaf ears.

She returned less than five minutes later, though the wait had seemed interminable. I didn't have to remind her to lock the door, glad to see she was as much on her toes as I was. "He says six-ten. Is that good?"

"It's not bad," I said. "But it's gonna be a bumpy ride. Are you sure you're up for it? I mean, I don't want to get you involved in something you might regret later on. You're a free agent. I don't want to force you to do anything."

"I said I'd do it and I will," she replied. "I haven't changed my mind. If you say you're innocent . . . well, I believe you. And that's all there is to it."

There was considerably more to it than that, needless to say. But I decided there was no sense worrying her unnecessarily. I looked at my watch. It was time to go. "Until we meet again, Miss Holmes," I said, purposely flip. She stood there, stiff and erect, holding her chin up so that she looked cocky and grim, all at once. I brushed her hair back away from her forehead, kissed her eyes and then her lips and finally stepped back.

"Please," she whispered. "Just . . . just don't get hurt."

"I'll try my best."

"The old college try?" and she forced herself to smile.

"You bet." Leaving my suitcase in her care, I winked and turned toward the door. Kate didn't move. When I looked back, she was staring at the tips of her fingers, that funny cockeyed little grin still managing to hold up under the strain. I slid the door back, made sure the corridor was deserted, and stepped outside, not stopping until I reached the john at the far end of the Pullman car. The other passengers were still asleep and the john was empty. I stepped inside and bolted the door behind me. Through the circular hole in the floor I could see the wooden crossties rushing by, sparks flying off the rails. The train was yet to decelerate, even though the Thazi depot couldn't be more than fifteen minutes away.

I pulled down the window, though it had nothing to do with the fact that the bathroom's odor was a definite health hazard. I hoisted myself up onto the edge of the grimy sill and crouched in readiness, my hands gripping the sides of the window frame, my knees pressed up against my chest. The pale green line of the horizon rose and fell in a gently undulating curve. Here and there the golden spires of Buddhist temples flashed by, glittering in the hazy morning light. Off in the distance a rooster crowed. Mist still blanketed the ground. It all added up to a picture postcard, a wish-you-were-here, a Technicolor travelogue filled with atmosphere and lots of local color.

"Thazi! Thazi!" the porter called out on the other side of the locked door.

I glanced out the window again, even as the train slowly began to lose speed. This is it, Carter. This is what your job's all about.

I held myself on the mark, as tightly coiled as a spring. And then I jumped as sky and ground did somersaults all around me. If you don't clear the tracks ... well, I thought, they'll just have to ship you home in a bamboo box and everyone'll remember what a nice guy you were.

The nice guy, everyone's favorite Killmaster N3, hit the

gravel shoulder, inches away from the iron rails. But I didn't stop there. I forced myself to keep rolling, bouncing and careening down a sloping incline, part of a shallow ravine that ran parallel to the tracks. Behind me the train roared by, still losing speed. The ground shook beneath me and a dozen stones started falling like hail. One hit my back, another my legs; a third glanced off my elbow, narrowly missing my head. Then everything slowly subsided, the noise, the flying rocks and stones, the earthquaking tremors.

One deep breath followed another as I lay still, waiting until the train was nothing more threatening than a distant rumble. A songbird trilled and warbled in the underbrush. The low and far-carrying "poo-poo-poo" of a hoopoe echoed softly in my ears. You said it, I thought. Then I raised my head and looked cautiously around, finally getting to my feet. I felt a little unsteady, woozy, like my legs were about to fold up beneath me. I was scratched and bruised but still in one piece, still in working order. No broken bones. No internal injuries. Just badly shaken up, but none the worse for wear.

"You'll get over it," I said aloud. "You'll survive ... just like always." The sound of my voice was oddly reassuring, almost comforting.

I looked around, trying to get my bearings.

As is often the case in my business, it was easier said than done.

Virtually impenetrable jungle confronted me wherever I turned my eyes. I had a detailed map of the area in my jacket pocket, but until I got to a road, it was going to be pretty much hit and miss. The shock hadn't bothered my watch, nor the roll of microfilm concealed within its stainless steel case. I dusted myself off, consulted my map, and started through the undergrowth. If the map was accurate, I'd eventually come out to a road—whatever that might mean—a mile or so on the other side of the jungle.

But traversing a mile of jungle is nothing like hiking

down a pleasant country lane. Branches whipped at my face as I made a path through the dense and dripping wet vegetation. I had to watch where my feet went, lest I upset any of Burma's more than two dozen species of poisonous and deadly snakes—kraits and cobras in particular. But it was worth all the trouble, just to know I had finally eluded my mysterious adversary, that unknown opponent I had dubbed—facetiously or not—Mr. X.

Even if he'd been on the train, it was obvious that his timing was off, just as it must have been when he showed up late at the National Museum. Rangoon seemed a thousand miles away, not three hundred. But now I had to reach a road in order to join up with what the map considered a "major highway," one that meandered in a gentle northwesterly direction, from Thazi to Meiktila, then across the Irrawaddy to the tiny and isolated village of Pagan.

So I kept at it. I'd already gotten my second wind and now the thought of leaving Burma—escaping, actually— was all the inducement I needed to keep going. But the dense tropical foliage seemed to check my progress, every step of the way. Lianas coiled and twisted like thick, fibrous snakes, tripping me up again and again. Rotting logs crisscrossed the path I was trying to make through the jungle. And always there lurked the omnipresent threat of venomous snakes. I can't say I was dressed for the occasion, either, though there was nothing I could do about that now. I just kept pressing forward, slowly but surely making progress through the wet and humid jungle.

It was well past seven when the undergrowth began to thin out. The dark-green of the interior lightened perceptibly. The morning haze had begun to lift and way in the distance there came back to me the sound of temple bells. I took my time now, not about to end up walking right into an ambush, a barricade thrown up by the government, the military. The creak of an oxcart rose above the stillness, while the aroma of dew-soaked grass wafted through the air like the most subtle and delicate of perfumes.

Too bad everything else isn't so peaceful, so idyllic, I thought.

Cautiously I stepped forward until there was hardly any ground cover, the thick vegetation giving way to low-growing shrubs and thorny bushes. I could see the road, just a scar across the jungle, a narrow track making its way through the interior. Crouching down, I consulted my map once again. If I headed due north, I'd reach the second road, one which ran roughly parallel to the railroad spur. It was here that Kate was supposed to meet me. According to the plan I'd worked out, the plan she'd agreed to follow, she was to hire a car in Thazi and then drive toward Meiktila, picking me up along the way. From there, we'd continue overland to Pagan, where I hoped to arrange for the hire of another car to take me across the border into Bangladesh. It was all too obvious that Rangoon was no longer a safe haven. It would be next to impossible to pass through customs at Mingaladon Airport. So I had no choice, no say in the matter. I'd have to make it through the Chin Hills district, some hundred and fifty miles across virtually unexplored territory, in order to reach the border outpost at Paletwa. But once I crossed over into Bangladesh, the bulk of my troubles would be over, my difficulties—and they were considerable, all right—a thing of the past.

So that was the scheme I'd worked out, some four or five hours earlier. If the plan succeeded and I managed to get safely out of Burma, I'd be able to rest easy, knowing that the requirements of the mission had been satisfied, fulfilled. But between Thazi and Paletwa any number of obstacles could present themselves. Smooth sailing may have been on the agenda, but there was no promise I'd have things easy from here on in.

All I could do was keep my eyes open and hope for the best.

I stepped out onto the road and turned right. The Rolex was equipped with a compass, so I knew I was heading in a northerly direction. I kept to the side of the dusty trail, just in case I had to duck out of sight. But no Jeeps or army vans rumbled down the narrow road. Perhaps they'd already given up, made their apologies to the Chinese, accepted the fact that I'd slipped through their fingers. It was a comforting thought, despite the fact that I really didn't give it too much credence. No, it would be foolish of me to lower my guard. Burma wasn't Boston, not by any stretch of the imagination. There was just no way to second-guess the authorities, whether they were civilian or military, or both.

The sun continued to rise, floating up high into the cloudless sky. Again, I heard the distant sound of Burmese gongs as I trudged down the road. If Kate didn't show up, I'd really be in bad shape. I didn't want to think about it. She'd gone along with me up to now, so why start worrying unnecessarily. Neither oxcart nor Jeep crossed my path. For thirty or forty minutes I continued at a steady pace, even as the sun started to beat down on me.

She'll be there, I kept telling myself. She's not going to disappoint me, not now, not when she knows how much I need her.

I reached the crossroad some two hours after I had jumped train. Covered with dust, my face scratched like a tick-tack-toe board, my clothes wet and rank with sweat, I was enough to scare anybody. But not Kate. She was sitting in the back seat of an old and battered saloon car, her eyes turned in the direction of the road along which I'd been hiking for the last forty minutes. The instant our eyes met she jumped out of the jeep and ran to meet me.

"Am I glad to see you!" she called out. "I've been sitting here worrying myself sick! I didn't know what to think, what to expect."

"Do you have water?" I whispered, my throat parched

and dry, my system well on its way to complete and total dehydration.

She nodded her head. "We brought along a canteen."

"We?"

"U San and I. He's the driver I found in Thazi. He's agreed to take us all the way into Pagan." She hooked her arm through mine and led me back to the Jeep. I slid into the back seat and took a long and grateful pull at the canteen, even as Kate went on a mile a minute, telling me it was distilled water, telling me how hard it had been to find a driver, let alone someone who owned a car.

"You ready to going now?" U San asked.

He looked back at us, a beetle-browed man somewhere in his early thirties, his one distinguishing feature being a milky eye, clouded over so that he was half-blind. It gave him an oddly sinister look, despite the fact that he was smiling at me from ear to ear.

"*Hoke ket,*" I said, nodding my head.

"*Ah lung kaung pa da,*" he replied. "We go now. Hokay?"

"Hokay," Kate said with a laugh. She snuggled up against me, looking as though she didn't have a care in the world. It was certainly a dramatic change from her attitude of the night before, when I'd found her standing in front of the baggage car, her eyes filled with shock and disbelief.

I leaned back against the seat and smiled to myself. U San turned the key in the ignition, released the emergency brake and put his foot on the gas. We were on our way.

I asked Kate to tell me what had happened, once she'd gotten off the train at Thazi.

"First of all, it was worse than you ever thought," she said. "Jeeps and armed soldiers, all kinds of officials milling about. Luckily they didn't go through my bags, because I got ahold of that customs officer—the one I gave the cigarettes to last night—and he helped me get through all the red tape." She glanced over her shoulder to where our suitcases were piled in the well behind the back seat. "Are we lucky they didn't open your bag?" she asked.

"Lucky?" I said, my forehead wrinkling up like a louver door. Unless I was misinterpreting the question, she seemed to still be under the illusion that I'd stolen something from the collection.

"You know what I mean," she said. She waved her hand in the air, trying to make light of my dismay.

"No, I honestly don't. There's nothing in it but my clothes," I replied. "But I guess it would have looked pretty funny if they found you walking around with some guy's wardrobe."

"Well, they didn't bother checking, so there's nothing to worry about," she said. She pretended to laugh.

"You still believe I'm a criminal, don't you?"

"That's not true. Just because I asked about your suitcase, doesn't mean—"

"Okay, let's drop it, Kate. You're here and that's what's most important."

"Thank you," she said. She avoided looking at me and went right into, "But finding someone with a car for hire ... that wasn't easy. Everyone in Thazi goes around on pony-carts, no kidding. I had to go to four different places before I met U San."

I turned my eyes back to the driver. He was staring straight ahead, both hands on the wheel. "Does he speak English?" I asked, lowering my voice.

"Not much," she said, catching my note of concern. "Just enough to get by. So you really don't have to watch what you say." She paused and smiled shyly. "Glad to see me?"

"More than you'd ever believe." I wasn't exaggerating, either.

"Good, I'm glad," she said, and put her head down on my shoulder. "But here I've been carrying on and I didn't even ask you how it went."

"I'm here. Right? It went okay. The hardest part was

jumping clear of the tracks. But after that, I just had to do a little more hiking than I'd planned on, that's all." I leaned forward and tapped U San on the shoulder. Through the rearview mirror I could see him looking up at me. "About how long do you think it'll take before we reach Pagan?" I asked.

"I no speaking very good English," he said.

I repeated the question in Burmese, immediately drawing out another one of his broad and toothy grins. "Seven hour maybe," he said, first in halting English and then in his own tongue. He kept his one good eye focused on the mirror.

"Thanks." When he looked away, I settled back in my seat and tried to unwind. Patience may be a virtue, as the old adage goes, but I felt antsy, unable to relax. Along the road I could see the smoke of cooking fires, rising up behind bamboo hedges which concealed small native compounds. But the locals didn't interest me as much as their militia. The conspicuous absence of anything even vaguely suggestive of law enforcement made me uneasy. Every bend in the road brought with it the threat of a barricade, an armed detachment of Burmese soldiers. Kate caught my anxious mood and straightened up in her seat, her playful, flirtatious attitude short-lived, evaporating into the steaming tropical air.

"You haven't told me what you plan to do, once we get to Pagan," she said.

"I'll see if I can convince U San to take me through the hills, across to the border."

"India?"

I shook my head. "Bangladesh is a little bit closer. I'll head for a place called Paletwa and hope for the best."

"I wish I understood what this was all about," she said with a loud and dispirited—exasperated, too—sigh. "You say you're innocent, but you're still running. I didn't mean anything bad about the suitcase, honest. But you can't run forever."

"You've been watching too much television," I told her, forcing myself to laugh. "Anyway, I don't intend to run forever, believe me. I just have to get out of Burma, that's all."

"That's all?" she exclaimed. She cocked her head to one side and eyed me curiously. "I just can't figure you out, Mr. Morley. I don't think I ever will."

She didn't say very much after that, which was just as well.

Round about three-thirty that afternoon I made out the brown muddy waters of the Irrawaddy. Pagan lay on the other side of the broad and slow-moving river, right in the heart of a dry and desolate plain which cut a wide swath across the center of Burma. The jungle and rice fields of Thazi and Meiktila had long since vanished. In their place the parched earth stretched out before us, as far as the eye could see.

"Look over there," Kate said. She pointed toward the river.

It was an eerie sight, all those deserted temples and lime-washed pagodas. They were set down like broken chess pieces, some five thousand monuments and ruins of monuments. All about us there seemed to settle a kind of preternatural calm, sad and timeless.

"It gives me the chills," Kate whispered, as if we were entering some kind of forbidden area, holy ground.

Only our driver, U San, seemed unimpressed with the view. He coasted slowly down a gently winding road until we were parked right by the edge of the river, narrow fishing boats moving back and forth from one side of the Irrawaddy to the other.

" 'Can't you 'ear their paddles chunkin' / from Rangoon to Mandalay? / On the road to Mandalay, / Where the flyin'-fishes play, / An' the dawn comes up like thunder / outer China 'crost the Bay!' "

Kate clapped her hands. "Thank you Joshua Morley . . ."

"Let's not forget Mr. Kipling," I said with a grin. "I mean, we might as well give credit where credit is due."

"Okay, thank you Rudyard Kipling, though his politics were enough to frighten even the most diehard . . . but isn't this a magical place? I've seen hundreds of photos, all kinds of drawings, illustrations. But to see it with your own eyes, to try to imagine what it must have looked like when King Anawratha ruled his empire, nine hundred years ago . . ." She shook her head, so moved that she couldn't even get the words out.

"And then Kubla Khan came along in 1287 and sacked the capital. And this is all that's left."

"But it's rich with history. Even if it's all deserted, crumbling into ruin, it's not really dead."

It made me smile to myself. I wanted to remember her just as she was now, the way she wore her feelings right on the tip of her finger, not the least bit ashamed to share her sense of awe, wonder. But finally I turned my eyes away and looked over at our driver. "What now, U San?"

"We taking ferry across river," he said. He pointed to the dock, just about visible from where we were parked.

"And then?" I asked.

He shrugged his shoulders, fixed his milky eye on me and said, "I not knowing. Is two places for staying in Pagan, but no one telling me which to go to."

"Kate, have you made any plans yet?"

"About what?"

"You know, room and board, sleeping arrangements," I explained. "After all, you're going to be staying here for the next five weeks. Didn't the government say anything about providing lodging?"

She shook her head. "No, I thought I'd take care of it once I arrived. Let me see what the guidebook says," she said, fishing her all-purpose guide to Burma out of one of her bags. She flipped through the pages until she found the information that we needed. "There are two places to stay," she told me. "One's a big modern hotel, fully air-conditioned. The Thiripyitsaya," she sputtered, stumbling over the name.

"How big is big?"

She consulted the book once again. "Twenty-four rooms."

"And the other one?"

"The other place is a UBA guest house, much more primitive . . . cheaper, too."

And probably a helluva lot safer and considerably more anonymous, I thought to myself. "I'd like to try the guest house, if it's all right with you."

"Sure. Whichever, it's fine with me."

"Guest house?" U San asked.

"Guest house it is."

We took two separate rooms, U San insisting he would sleep in his car and just join us for meals.

Even though Kate and I were the only tourists currently in residence at the guest house, I still didn't feel completely relaxed or confident enough to breathe easy. Nevertheless, it seemed highly improbable that the military would be looking this far afield, having no reason to suspect that the man who "ransacked" the baggage car would end up in Pagan. After all, the village consisted of little more than a market, a school, and the woven bamboo houses of some three thousand people. Other than that, and the new hotel, the ruins dominated the scene. For sixteen miles they stretched along a curve of the river, some with stupas covered with tiny squares of gold leaf, others of a white that was almost blinding to the eye.

I didn't bother unpacking. A quick, cold shower and a change of clothes and I felt civilized again. Kate suggested we use whatever daylight remained to take a look at some of the ruins. That was fine with me, because I wanted to get a chance to talk to U San. The manager of the guest house had told me there were only two Jeeps for hire in all of Pagan, but that they never left the immediate area. Since U San had traveled with us all the way from Thazi,

I hoped my powers of persuasion would be able to convince him to continue overland until I reached the border.

He drove us to the Shwezigon pagoda, its entire surface overlaid with countless squares of gold leaf. Kate disappeared inside, leaving me alone with our driver. "I'm interested in going on to Paletwa," I told him, speaking in Burmese so that there wouldn't be any question of what I had in mind.

"Paletwa is very far," he said. "The roads are very bad. It will not be an easy journey."

"I'm prepared to pay you very well for your troubles."

He rubbed his bare toes in the sand and kept his eyes glued to the ground. "How much you pay?" he said in English.

"Name your price."

He did, and by Western standards it was still very cheap.

"Will we have trouble getting gasoline?" I asked. "Petrol?"

"Not so bad. I have extra ... how you say, tanks in car."

"Then we have a deal, U San. We'll be leaving tomorrow morning, how's that?"

"Hokay," and we shook on it.

DAY FIVE—fifth day of seven allowed by the Burmese government.

It was duck eggs and glutinous rice, all over again.

Sitting alone in the guest house dining room, I was trying to figure out a way to say good-bye to Kate. I wanted her to know how grateful I was for all that she had done. She'd put herself on the line for me and that was something I didn't take lightly. I wanted to tell her how I felt about it, the fact that she'd put her trust in someone whom she really didn't know very well, a total stranger only once or twice removed.

But until she joined me for breakfast and took her place at the table, there was no way to tell her anything. I picked at my food, my system yet to fully recover from my fruit-eating binge. The village was as awake as I was. On the other side of the dining room windows I could see the women making their first trip to the well. Life went on, basically unchanged from one century to the next. I glanced at my watch. It was already seven-thirty and I wanted to get started by eight, at the very latest. U San had said it would take two days to reach the border because of the poor condition of the roads. The greater the distance I put between myself and Rangoon, the happier I'd be. I had the microfilm, but now I had to make sure it got out of the country and into safe hands.

I poured myself another cup of tea. Hurrying footsteps reached my ears. U San suddenly came into view. He was out of breath, his forehead dotted with beads of sweat. He put both hands on the table and stared at me intently, his one good eye opening wide with excitement.

"She's not there," he gasped, barely able to get the words out.

I started from my seat. "What do you mean, she's not there? Miss Holmes isn't in her room, is that it?"

He nodded his head and pointed behind him, his arm jerking out in the direction of the cubicles where Kate and I had spent the night. "I knocked on the door and when she didn't answer I let myself in and ... it was empty," he said in Burmese.

"She must have gone out to get some air or ... or something," I said, trying to calm him down, myself as well. Nevertheless, I followed him out of the dining room, past a wicker-furnished lounge, and then to a wide corridor lined by cubicles. The door to Kate's room was still ajar. I pushed it open and stepped inside, U San right on my heels.

I didn't like what I saw.

The room was in complete and total disarray, and not

because Kate Holmes was a sloppy person, either. No, it
had nothing to do with personal neatness, or the lack of
it. The lamp near the bed had been knocked onto the
floor and dresser drawers had been pulled out, Kate's belongings strewn about the room. The single window near
the metal dresser, one which looked out onto the rear of
the guest house, was opened wide. When I saw that the
wire screen had been removed, I had a sinking feeling
that Kate hadn't gone out for either a breath of air or her
morning constitutional.

If we've been followed, I thought to myself.

I didn't want to finish the sentence, accept the fact that
I'd been outsmarted by a man I'd never even seen before.
"Was the room like this a few minutes ago?" I asked U
San.

"Yes," he said. "The same."

My eyes continued to take in everything at once, even
as I began to move around the room. I was still hoping
there might be some kind of logical explanation for the
complete and total disorder. But when I saw a scrap of
paper fluttering up and down on top of the dresser, no
amount of optimism could overcome my mounting fears
for Kate's safety. I snagged it with two fingers. The lipsticked note was short and to the point:

MANAHA TEMPLE HE HAS A GUN.

"You have gas in the car?" I said, turning quickly to
the driver.

His head bobbed up and down. "Is trouble?"

There was no reason to lie. "It looks that way," I said,
cursing myself for having allowed Kate to become involved in my affairs.

Everything I'd been afraid of now seemed to have already taken place, right under my nose. Unless I was way
off the track, Kate had been hustled out of her room at
gunpoint. No doubt she would be held captive until such
time as I gave up all rights to the microfilm, bartering the
spy list for her life. Whoever had been responsible for

murdering Poy Chu and Wai Tsang obviously wouldn't hesitate to take a third life if they didn't get what they wanted.

"Do you know how to get us to the Manaha temple?"

U San thought for a moment and then nodded his head. "We go now?"

"Yep, we go now." I followed him outside to the Jeep, Wilhelmina ready to be put to use should Mr. X's scenario dictate that kind of violent and drastic action.

It was hot and dry and as still as death. U San got behind the wheel as I swung into the back seat. What had seemed a foolproof scheme had rapidly become riddled with holes. And now I was heading for a confrontation I had hoped to avoid, all along. Unfortunately, there was nothing I could do about it. Kate was gone and as long as her life was hanging in the balance, I had to do whatever I could to help her. I just hoped I wouldn't be too late.

The road we took was dusty and deserted. The Jeep bounced over the ruts while on either side rice paddies and desolate ruins met my narrowed and watchful eyes. Somewhere out there an automatic was being held in readiness. Somewhere in that complex of shattered monuments Kate Holmes was being used as a pawn. The chessmaster had called the shot, made his move. Now, it was my turn to make sure it was checkmate, and as soon as possible.

The village was lost in a cloud of dust as U San drove at breakneck speed in the direction of the temple. How the hell did he follow us? I kept asking myself, still finding it hard to believe that my mysterious adversary had managed to stay on my trail, even after I'd jumped train back near Thazi. For once his timing must have been letter-perfect, because he hadn't had any trouble catching up to me, even less trouble kidnapping Kate. I'd warned her it was going to be a bumpy ride, but I never expected it to be this bumpy.

Or this dangerous.

U San turned off the dirt road and followed a narrow and overgrown path that led out into the center of a rice field, a patch of dark-green in what was otherwise a desolate and arid plain. I could see the Manaha in the distance, a multitiered wedding cake of white and gold. Set down in the middle of nowhere, it was like a citadel, a fortress of balconies and turrets, narrow stairways and blind, labyrinthine passages.

The Jeep rolled across the empty field, slowly losing speed until U San eased down on the brakes. We came to an abrupt and sudden stop, a good hundred yards from the entrance to the abandoned temple. I kept down as I slid out of the back seat, using the Jeep as a shield while I searched the blind eyes of the monument: square stone-sided windows which looked out on the surrounding fields. A pair of sacred lions of plaster and brick stood guard before the temple, silent and watchful, all-knowing.

"Stay down, out of sight," I whispered to U San.

In an instant he had joined me on the other side of the saloon car. At least he wasn't asking any questions, following my instructions without so much as a moment's hesitation. I kept my eyes on the front of the temple and decided to chance it. Without saying another word I dashed across the open field, not about to stop until I'd reached one of the two lions I'd noticed a minute or so earlier.

The figure provided me with adequate cover, while I continued to search out the openings in the temple wall. Any second and I had a feeling I'd see the glint of metal, the barrel of a revolver catching the morning light as it was leveled in my direction. But nothing moved and nothing glittered, save for the faded gold leaf still adhering to the topmost turrets and balustrades of the long-abandoned monument.

He's got to be in there somewhere, I thought. "Kate!" I called out. "Kate, are you in there!"

Perhaps my party hadn't even seen the Jeep pulling up

in front of the temple. Perhaps he still was waiting for me to arrive, not yet aware of the fact that I was already there. I was anxious to put an end to the business he'd started, less than an hour before. But until I could see who I was dealing with, I couldn't do very much of anything.

That's when I saw the tire tracks.

They led right toward the entrance to the temple and then doubled back, heading in the direction from which I'd just come with U San, the UBA guest house and the village of Pagan. Without stepping out from behind the brick and plaster lion, I leaned forward and tried to examine the tracks more carefully. I could just about make out the details of the treads, but not much more than that.

Nevertheless, one look was all I needed. I threw myself forward then, not about to be a sitting duck for anyone. A wild zigzagging run brought me back—breathless but unharmed—to the safety of the Jeep. I made it around to the other side of the vehicle and glanced down at the tracks left by U San's battered saloon car. They were identical to the tracks I'd seen not two minutes earlier.

Without thinking twice about it I reached for Wilhelmina.

"I wouldn't do that if I were you, Mr. Carter." It was U San, his English as flawless as the nickeled finish of his Hi-Standard Snub Barrel Sentinel. It was a .357 Magnum, and unless I was mistaken, Wilhelmina was about to be outclassed.

CHAPTER THIRTEEN

"You look a little ... shaken up, Mr. Carter," U San went on, his cloudy opaque eye wide and unblinking. His .357 Magnum was leveled on my chest, his finger tight against the trigger guard.

"Let's just say I'm surprised, U San, and leave it at that." I smiled gamely and took one step to the side so the sun wouldn't be in my eyes.

U San reacted immediately. His index finger slid off the trigger guard and caressed the trigger proper. A little more passion and it would be all over. "Don't do that again, Mr. Carter," he advised with a smug and self-satisfied grin. "It makes me very nervous. And when I'm nervous, all sorts of nasty things can happen."

I held my tongue, all eyes to his revolver.

"A snug little package, is she not?" he asked and chuckled to himself. "American-made, I might add. And quite powerful, particularly at such a short distance."

"Where's Kate?"

"Miss Holmes?" He screwed up his one good eye and glanced over at the Manaha. "She is out of harm's way, perfectly safe. But if you want to see her again, Mr. Carter ... alive, that is ... all you need do is hand over the film. It's really as simple as that."

It was considerably more complicated, but I wasn't about to get into an argument over semantics. So this is the bastard who's been biting my ass, ever since I set foot in Hong Kong. Unbelievable, and a Burmese national, on top of everything else. It was mind-boggling, disconcerting, to put it mildly.

"Well?" he snapped. "The film, Mr. Carter."

He was so hot to get his hands on the spy list that he seemed to have forgotten about Wilhelmina, half-in and half-out of her holster. I kept my hands by my sides and hoped he had a short attention span. "I don't have it with me," I said, returning his cool and unemotional stare.

"You're lying."

"No, afraid not," I said. "I left it back at the guest house. In a safe place, of course. Just like Kate. But I had no intention of carrying it around like ... a bag of peanuts."

"Your metaphor is neither amusing nor instructive, Mr. Carter. Should I squeeze the trigger, I will have all the time I require to make a complete and thorough search. And if I should discover that you weren't lying, that you were telling me the truth, well ... it'll just be too late for me to make amends. So let's avoid further difficulties. The film, if you please."

"And Kate?" I asked, stalling for time while I tried to figure out how to get around him.

"I told you, she is still alive. You will see her again, rest assured."

"I just want to know that she's in better shape than Poy Chu and Wai Tsang."

U San said nothing, absolutely nothing at all.

"So you want the film," I finally went on.

"Yes, and I'm getting quite impatient, Carter," he replied. "Where is it, or would you prefer a bullet to begin my interrogation?"

I shook my head. "No, I'd hate that to happen. It's much too nice a day for bloodshed."

He neither laughed nor frowned, his Sentinel as steady as a proverbial rock. A mere flick of his trigger finger and I'd have a porthole through my midsection. It wasn't what you'd call a comforting thought.

"You'll tell me where Kate is if I hand over the film? Is that a promise?"

"A promise."

"Well, I guess you've got the draw on me." I bent forward and reached for my left shoe. "The heel is hollow," I explained, just in case he was getting unduly nervous. I pretended to have a lot of trouble pulling off the shoe. U San stood over me. His face was like a mask, holding neither clues nor answers.

But instead of removing my calfskin loafer, I suddenly scooped up a handful of dirt and flung it in the agent's eyes. Momentarily blinded, U San didn't hesitate to squeeze the trigger. The shot went wild and I lunged forward, trying to tackle him so that he'd lose his footing. He was as nimble as a goat, easily sidestepping me as my outstretched hands met air, not agent. I threw myself back and then rolled sideways to get out of the line of fire. I had to reach the other side of the Jeep in order to avoid getting my head blown off. A second shot rang out, the bullet sending up a cloud of dust as it ricocheted less than a foot away from me. I threw up more dirt and crawled forward, right beneath the undercarriage of the saloon car.

I could see U San's feet. He was wearing shoes, as opposed to going around barefoot, as he did the day before. The cracked leather shoes and the cuffs of a pair of baggy, flapping trousers stepped hurriedly back. I reached for Wilhelmina, thankful that U San hadn't asked me to disarm, a few minutes earlier. But when I leveled her sights on my opponent, his shoes and baggy pants were no longer in my line of vision.

Pulling myself around beneath the Jeep, I turned in the direction of the deserted temple. The Burmese ducked out of sight behind one of the plaster lions, getting off another round of gunfire. If he wasn't careful he'd blow out the tires of his car. But I didn't have the time or inclination to remind him to take better aim. Rather, I inched back until I could once again feel the morning sun beating down on me. I got quickly to my feet and crouched behind the nearest fender, the Jeep providing me with ample cover.

The Snub Barrel Sentinel, possibly the meanest 3½ inches in anybody's arsenal, flashed like a semaphor from behind the edge of the mute and centuries-old lion. The high-caliber slug struck the rusty hood of the Jeep and seemed to split in two like shrapnel.

The instant I heard the staccato crack of U San's automatic, I raised Wilhelmina and aligned her sights, front and rear. Then I squeezed down on the trigger. The lion lost an ear as U San tried to scramble to safety. His .357 spit fire with an eardrum-shattering drone of red-hot lead. I started to my feet, giving Wilhelmina all the play and freedom she seemed to be demanding.

I managed to get off another round before he ducked inside the temple. By this time I was crouched between the Jeep and the plaster lion. I rushed forward, trying to make it to the figure before U San got a chance to demonstrate his marksmanship. The revolver glinted for an instant, followed by another sharp report as he squeezed the trigger. I made it to the lion, but not before his slug had done its damage. The pain was like a firebrand, the bullet having creased my shoulder. It must have plowed clear through my sleeve, coming out on the other side. Even as I dropped down so he wouldn't be able to continue his deadly game of target-practice, I was pulling off my torn and dusty blazer.

My shirt-sleeve was saturated with blood, a bright fiery red where once it had been a sea island blue. I tore at the sleeve until it came free, exposing the deep and nasty track of U San's .357 Magnum. The slug had tunneled through the outer muscle, leaving in its wake a raw and bloodied wound. My arm was already tingling, growing increasingly numb with each passing second. Unless I managed to stop the copious bleeding, I'd be in no condition to continue after U San, in no shape to help Kate, either.

The first thing I did was to tie the torn sleeve around the wound, bandaging it as best I could. Next, I unbuckled my slim alligator belt and pulled it free of the trouser loops. Rapidly I fashioned a makeshift tourniquet, using the belt and a ballpoint pen to stanch the flow of blood. The pen served the function of a screw, keeping the belt tight around my upper arm. As long as I didn't forget to loosen it every five or ten minutes or so, I'd be in pretty good shape. And since I was ambidextrous—trained that way, I might add—it didn't matter which arm had taken the fall. Wilhelmina was as perfectly comfortable in my left hand as she was in my right.

U San had disappeared inside the temple and now I waited, searching the darkened and shadow-filled entranceway for another glimpse of his nickel-plated Sentinel. But neither the .357 Magnum nor his blind white eye could be seen, emerging out of the shadows to send another lightning bolt of lead screaming and hissing in my direction. So I had no choice. I had to get to him before he got to Kate. And if he'd already reached her, then I had to do some pretty fancy footwork or else I'd have a corpse on my hands.

It wasn't what you'd call a happy thought, or a particularly pleasant situation, either.

In order to reach the temple, I would have to break from cover. If the driver was still lurking by the entrance, I wouldn't stand a chance in the world. I reached down and picked up a fist-sized stone I found at my feet. Then, transferring my Luger to my right hand, I heaved the stone in the direction of the desolate and crumbling shrine. I could hear the rock strike the ground with a dull, echoing thud. If U San was waiting on the other side of the entrance, he was a helluva lot cooler than I would have thought. The falling missile hadn't made him trigger-happy and I decided it was time to make my move.

As dangerous as it would be, it was also absolutely necessary. Even now Kate might have the Snub Barrel at her head, a weapon whose owner had already demonstrated both his deadly skill with sidearms and his lack of inhibition when it came to pulling the plug on someone's life.

I sure as hell didn't want to see her short-circuited, certainly not when I felt responsible for her safety, her wellbeing, her very life.

So I ran.

It was as simple and risky as that.

I started from my hiding place, bursting into view like a target in a penny arcade. But neither U San nor his .357 could be seen as I raced across the open courtyard. Just as I reached the entrance to the temple, he let loose another round. The shot came from on high, above me, somewhere inside the building. He might have been taking aim from any number of terraces, porticos which looked out on the surrounding countryside.

The gunshot wound still burned as if someone was holding a match to my flesh. I loosened the tourniquet, caught my breath and gave my eyes a chance to grow accustomed to the diminished light. The interior of the Manaha consisted of narrow passageways of hand-hewn stone. Dust covered the earthen floor, while statues of Buddha stood, reclined, and sat cross-legged within numerous architectural niches, recesses which had been carved out of the surrounding stone walls. One of the clay statues had been recently painted. The Buddha it portrayed sported garish red lips and coal-black eyes. It seemed to watch me as I tried to decide which corridor to follow. But since it didn't come up with any concrete suggestions, I turned right and kept Wilhelmina in readiness, my back flat against the dusty stone wall of the passage.

I edged forward, trying to pierce the shadows with my narrowed eyes. The 900-year-old monument afforded countless hiding places. Any moment and I expected U San to show his stuff, either his single good eye or his

Hi-Standard automatic. But neither the blink of an eye nor the glint of a snub-nosed revolver came into view. I continued down the passage until I reached a stone stairway which led up to the next level of the temple.

The steps were uneven. Some slanted up while others buckled under my weight and threatened to give way. It was impossible to stand erect, as though the stairway had been designed for a child. I glanced up and saw how some of the cobwebs had been pulled aside. U San must have been here a few minutes before and I moved more cautiously than ever, having no idea what I might find when I reached the landing at the top of the stairs.

The sun suddenly came into view, streaming through a semicircular, windowlike opening in the side of the Manaha. I could see U San's footprints now, clearly visible in the thick carpet of dust which covered the stone steps. They wound up and up and I took them one at a time, my Luger held at arm's length before me like some kind of beacon, a candle to show me the way.

Then U San finally gave himself away and I was taking the stairs two at a time. The echo of running footsteps resounded in my ears. I reached the top of the stairway and ducked back, able to catch sight of a single billowing trouser leg. Now that I knew he hadn't gotten to Kate, I didn't hesitate to hurry after him down the dust-choked corridor. Swinging around a right-angle bend in the hall, I proceeded up another and equally narrow flight of winding and rickety stone stairs.

The darkness of the first level was now replaced by a dim though evenly distributed illumination. When I got to the top of the second flight of steps I could see how the third level of the Manaha was ringed by terraces which jutted out on every side, much like our latter-day widow's walks. Not six inches from where I was standing, the stone wall seemed to explode in a blinding cloud of dust. Flying sharp-edged chips of splintered rock were scattered at my feet as another one of U San's cartridges left its mark on the ancient monument.

With a jerk I was stumbling back toward the safety of the stairs, my eyes frantically searching for a sign, some flurry of movement, which would enable me to locate and hence pinpoint my adversary. If the balconies were contiguous, he might just be circling around, determined to end my stay in Burma with a single burst of gunfire and a bullet lodged in my back.

I had no intention of allowing that to happen.

Again, I paused just long enough to loosen the tourniquet. The bullet wound was still bleeding, though less copiously than before. I waited fifteen or twenty seconds and once again used the pen to screw the belt tight. Then, wiping my bloodstained hands on my trousers so that I'd be able to keep a firm grip on Wilhelmina, I crept forward until I reached the nearest terrace.

It was flooded with white light, while beyond the stone balustrade stretched a blasted plain of ruins and rice paddies. The Irrawaddy sparkled in the distance, a faint brown ribbon meandering across the horizon.

I turned my head from left to right, trying to catch sight of U San. Apparently he wasn't taking any chances, because the balcony was empty. The winds had swept away the dust. So there weren't any tracks to lead me in the right direction.

"U San!" I called out. "Let's make a deal. I just want the girl. Tell me where she is and I'll give you the film!"

His voice came from behind me. I swung around and confronted thin air. "You're lying," he yelled back, reverting to his native Burmese.

"Just tell me where she is and the film is yours," I said again. I still couldn't see him, but I sure as hell wasn't about to step out into the middle of the terrace, there to be picked off *hana-dool-set*, one-two-three.

He didn't answer.

I could hear the blood pounding in my temples, hear

the far off whisper of bells and gongs, carried by the breeze. A bird whose plumage was as red as my bloodied shirt-sleeve landed on one of the terrace railings. It shuffled its tail feathers as if it was dealing cards. Then it took off again, the instant another slug whistled angrily through the air. I spun around and squeezed the trigger.

My 9mm Luger wasn't outclassed, after all.

U San's Hi-Standard Sentinel did a wild, whirling dance as it flew from his fingers. It bounced off one stone wall and then another, even as I stepped forward, keeping Wilhelmina trained on the man who'd been dogging my tracks for just about as long as I'd been in Asia. "I like these new rules much better," I told him. "And I'll like them even more, once you tell me where Kate is."

"As they say in your country, that is for me to know and you to guess."

I didn't say a word after that.

Stepping closer, I grabbed hold of U San's arm and pulled him forward, out of the narrow passage. With the sun full upon his face, his skin still looked washed out, drained of color. His lips were pursed, his single blinking eye studying me as intently as a scientist hunched over a microscope, examining a specimen. Suddenly his eye flicked away, back in the direction of the stone-walled passage. I must have turned my head for all of a second, but U San knew an opening when he saw one.

As fast as my karate master, he reached out and grabbed me around the waist, deflecting Wilhelmina's barrel so that she was aimed at his feet, not his chest. I sent my left leg snapping forward, but U San knew his moves as well as I did. He jerked to the side and still holding onto my gun hand, now let loose with a piercing-hand attack. The *pyon-sohn-koot* forced me to stumble backwards, lest I find my eyes rolling on the terrace floor like a pair of marbles. Again I tried a snapping front kick, only to meet his own foot as it came crashing into my arm.

The pain was like a hundred shredded nerves, each one

being ripped and torn in unison. Even though I tried to keep my fingers tight around Wilhelmina, U San's kick made them involuntarily relax. The Luger dropped to my feet and there just wasn't time to retrieve her. Right then and there the Burmese came plowing into me with both hands raised. It was *a-le ji-lu-ki* and *a-le mak-ki*, *mom-tong ji-lu-ki* and *mom-tong mak-ki*. Punch and block, punch and block, trying to divert his menacing fists from slamming first into my groin, then my throat.

"We even now!" he called out, his lips pulled back in a wicked and all too self-satisfied grin. He swiveled lightly on the ball of his foot and thrust his leg out in a round kick to my kidney.

In turn, I slid one step forward and blocked it as best I could, slamming my left forearm away from my side so that the kick landed on my inner arm, not my considerably more vulnerable kidney. But that didn't stop him. Jerking back like a windup toy, he didn't waste time as he lashed out with a right forward kick. I parried with a double block, both hands together, one over the other. The heel of his shoe slammed into my wrist and I gritted my teeth and stepped back. The tourniquet was loosening up and blood was starting to trickle down from the bullet wound in my shoulder. The pain was becoming unbearable now and unless I switched from the defensive to the offensive, I knew that soon I wouldn't have the use of either arm.

In a last-ditch effort to get the upper hand, I poised on the ball of one foot and then threw myself forward. The leaping kick saw my instep collide with U San's chin. His head was thrown viciously back and he skipped away, a dozen or more steps. The one thing he wasn't aware of was that he was coming closer and closer to the balusters and railing which ringed the terrace. I had no intention of easing up, not when he kept shaking his head as though he couldn't get his equilibrium. I rushed forward, fists raised, my right foot swinging out in a high and deadly arc. He tried to sidestep the roundhouse, but the *tol rio cha-ki* just couldn't be blocked. My foot slammed into his temple and U San was thrown back until he was hanging against the balustrade like a punch-drunk fighter playing the ropes.

A side kick to the solar plexus and he clutched at his stomach. One second he looked pale and the next his pallor was replaced by a sick and nauseated green. And a moment after that, U San was spraying his breakfast across the balcony floor. I had both hands on his throat then, trying not to think of the pain or the way blood kept sluicing down my arm.

"Where is she!" I barked, shaking him back and forth against the railing.

U San looked up at me, the lower part of his face one swollen and purpling bruise. Then his knee came up with such speed and force that there just wasn't any way to avoid it.

It was a kick in the balls, in every sense of the word.

Unable to help myself, I let go of his throat and jumped back, trying—and failing—to stop myself from doubling up with pain. There seemed to be no air in my lungs, my groin crushed, the terrace spinning around me as I reeled and shook my head and reeled some more. I could see Wilhelmina, still where I'd dropped her on the other side of the balcony. I staggered toward my Luger, only to feel U San's foot slamming across the small of my back. Knocked forward, flat on my face, I started dragging myself along the stone floor.

But Wilhelmina was just too far away.

He was on top of me then and with a flick of my wrist I had Hugo in my one good hand. The razor-sharp stiletto caught the light, caught the reflection of U San's astonished expression. He lunged for the knife as I twisted over onto my back and slashed out. The point of the stiletto went clear through his white and sightless eye.

U San gave a scream of animal pain. His savage rage

turned into a single, unending shriek that seemed to claw at his throat. He tried to pull away from me as the blade of the knife continued to jerk back and forth as though it had a life of its own. I yanked it free of its slippery mooring and one side of his face was now encrusted with blood and gore as he kept on screaming, unable to bear the blinding pain that was his disfigured and butchered face.

Shakily I got back on my feet, Hugo still in my hand. I caught hold of the trailing end of my belt, gripped it between my teeth and pulled it tight, once again stanching the flow of blood. I was weak, dizzy and barely able to maintain my balance or my footing. U San was still stepping back, one hand cupped over the gelatinous slivers that were once an eye.

"Where is she?" I said again, gasping as I tried to fill my lungs with air.

Instead of answering he reached down and fumbled with the cuff of his grimy and bloodstained trousers. Another metallic reflection caught the harsh morning light as he rushed toward me, swinging a gem blade like a scythe, slashing back and forth through the air.

I sidestepped out of the way and sent Hugo whistling across the terrace. The stiletto caught U San right between his shoulder blades. He stumbled and clawed at his back with one hand, refusing to relinquish his hold on the razor blade.

No wonder they're in such short supply, I heard myself thinking.

Without hesitating any longer, I bounded toward him and slammed Hugo in, right up to the hilt. He was at the railing now, gripping the stone balustrade with both hands. He kicked back like a bronco, refusing to give up, even as a thick stream of blood seeped through his thin cotton shirt.

"It's all over, buddy," I said and pulled Hugo free, grabbed hold of one of U San's jerking legs and pushed him forward.

He didn't even scream.

One minute he was there and the next he was gone. I looked over the edge of the parapet and then turned my eyes away just as quickly. U San lay at the foot of the Manaha, smashed and broken.

I leaned against the railing and tried to clear my head. First the tourniquet, I thought, retying the blood-soaked shirt-sleeve before adjusting the makeshift belt and pen arrangement. Then I retrieved Wilhelmina and slipped her back inside her holster. She'd seen more than enough action for one day. I put Hugo away as well, wiping the blade clean before sliding the stiletto into its chamois sheath.

U San's Sentinel, I remembered.

I turned toward the passage which led back inside the temple. There was still a lot to be done. First and foremost, I had to find Kate. Then U San's body had to be disposed of before we drove back to Pagan.

Just take everything one step at a time, I told myself.

But the Sentinel wasn't where U San had dropped it, where Wilhelmina had clipped it neatly across its deadly, snub-nosed barrel.

Come on, I thought, a gun just doesn't disappear into thin air.

I bent down and searched the floor of the passageway. I didn't want to leave any evidence behind, any clues that there had been a skirmish—nice word that, but not very descriptive of what I'd just gone through—at the Manaha temple.

Well, at least the worst is over. Right?

Wrong.

The worst wasn't over, not by a long shot.

You see, I found U San's Hi-Standard, his .357 Magnum, all right. But it wasn't lying on the dusty floor of the passage. It was attached to a hand, a hand whose slim index finger now tickled its trigger with a light and gentle touch, delicate though far from subtle. The hand was attached to a shoulder and the shoulder attached to a svelte and arousing body. I looked up and tried to smile.

"You've had a very busy morning—Nick Carter."

"It looks like it's gonna get even busier ... Kate Holmes."

CHAPTER FOURTEEN

"Surprised?"

"Very," I admitted, remembering how she'd said that once before, back in the dining room of the Strand.

"It was fun while it lasted though, wasn't it."

"*Fun* just doesn't seem to do it justice, Kate," I replied, all eyes to the Sentinel, all eyes to the set and determined look around her lips, her glacier-cool blue eyes. "I always thought the eyes were wrong," I said aloud. "Now I know why."

"Wrong?"

I nodded my head. "Shallow, a little too cool for comfort. A little too hard for the nice girl next-door, the all-American archaeologist."

"Actually, that was my field of study, believe it or not."

"Was?"

"Before ... before I realized that past history wasn't nearly as important as present history, or the history of the future. And its going to be a glorious future, and sooner than anyone realizes. It's just unfortunate there has to be ... violence along the way, that's all."

I pointed behind me, even as I stepped back until I was standing on the terrace, bathed in sunlight. "Tell that to your partner," I said. "He wanted to fly, just like Leonardo. Only problem, he didn't have wings."

"He gave his life for the cause," she said. She took her time, moving slowly forward to join me on the balcony which overlooked the ruins of Pagan, the blood-red ruin that was the shattered and twisted body of U San.

"And what cause is that, Kate?"

"Freedom for oppressed peoples, the world over," she replied with robotlike precision. She held her chin up and her shallow blue eyes flashed a blend of pride and defiance.

"You've been brainwashed."

" 'fraid not. I just got wise to myself, that's all. The liberal wants to help the oppressed, because he has a guilty conscience. The true revolutionary realizes he's *part* of the oppressed, unfree."

"You and the Symbionese . . ."

"I just want the film, Nick."

"What makes you think I have it?"

She threw her head back and laughed, deliberately scornful. I'd never heard that laugh before. It seemed to come from somewhere inside her where I'd never been, never seen, never known. It was as cool as her eyes and as brittle as her tightly pursed lips. Kate had thrown aside the mask she'd worn ever since we first met. In its place I now faced a young woman whose consummate cunning had taken me completely by . . . yes, there was that word again. Surprise. She'd taken me completely and totally by surprise.

"Keep your hands up," she said, her mood darkening. Her finger tightened against the trigger. I raised my hands above my head. "Very good. Now I want you to take hold of your gun with two fingers . . . two fingers, Nick. Not three or four or else I pull the trigger, and I've done it before so please don't push me. Take hold of your gun with two fingers and drop it to the floor. Is that clear?"

"Crystal clear." I did precisely what she told me, not the least bit uncertain as to her ability to send a heavy caliber slug screaming through the air, screaming through my guts. Wilhelmina clattered to the floor. Once again I raised my hands above my head, hoping against hope she didn't see the outline of Hugo's chamois sheath, just about visible beneath the fabric of my lightweight shirt.

"And now the microfilm, Nick."

"It's yours," I told her. "After all . . . you've earned it. You've done brilliantly. Your boss'll probably want to pin a medal on your beautiful chest." I was cursing Kate, but cursing myself even more for having fallen for her charms, for having put my trust in her. There was a lesson there, invaluable, one that I was not about to ever forget . . . if I survived Pagan, that is, if Kate's .357 Magnum didn't put an end to my . . . illustrious career.

"I have no boss," she said at last, avoiding my narrowed and searching eyes. It was as if she feared her new mask would come undone and once again she'd find herself back in the role of Marian Librarian. "I work for the people."

"What kind of people? The same people who murdered Poy Chu and that guy on the hydrofoil, Wai Tsang?"

"Poy Chu was a traitor to the cause," she said. "But I didn't have anything to do with that. Someone else . . . botched the job. He wasn't supposed to be killed. He was supposed to be brought back to—" She stopped abruptly and looked away.

"Peking?"

"I want the roll of film, Nick. That's all that counts. I know it's not in your suitcase . . . or its hidden compartment."

"You checked?"

"Of course I checked," she said with rising impatience. "Do you take me for a fool?"

"No, that's the one thing you're obviously not," I replied. "But at least give me the benefit of a couple of answers. That's all I'm asking, Kate. I told you, the film is yours. I know when I'm licked. But I just want to know—"

"Who killed Wai Tsang?" she said, filling in one of the blanks.

"Yes."

"I couldn't allow him to give my cover away. I had no choice."

"And you were at the museum, back in Rangoon, weren't you?"

"I got there when the alarms started going off . . ."

"That's what I figured. But why didn't you just have the attaché conduct a search of the artifacts? You knew Poy Chu had hidden the film with the exhibit, didn't you?"

"We didn't know that until the break-in," she said. "But I don't want to answer any more questions, Nick. Let's just say I was instructed to . . . kill two birds with one stone, and leave it at that."

One bird being the spy list, the other the spy, I thought. "Just two more questions, and that'll be the end of it," I told her. "U San, for starters."

"A local contact, who died for the cause," she repeated, parroting the rhetoric of the party line, word for word.

I just couldn't hack it: the way she'd changed; the way she was operating, as dispassionate as a machine. "How in God's name did they convince you of all this, Kate?"

"God had nothing to do with it," she said without missing a beat.

Again I raised my voice, trying to get through to her. "What did they put you through?" It was all so inconceivable, so difficult to believe that she was Mr. X, the person I'd been trying to outwit all this time.

"They didn't put me through anything," she said, her expression at once hard and unfeeling, completely devoid of emotion. "But since you're so interested, it all started about three years ago, while I was attending an international archaeology conference in Stockholm. And if you want to know why a nice girl like me—and if that doesn't smack of sexism and male chauvinism, I don't know what does—got into such an . . . unusual line of work, the answer is really quite simple. A very special person was killed, gunned down, murdered by—"

"Pigs?" I said with a bitter laugh.

"By men who have no idea how oppressed they are," she replied. "Remember Ohio? Kent State? May fourth, 1970?"

"It was something no one wanted, Kate," I said, still trying to reason with her. "But I'm sorry, believe me I am."

"Don't be, Mr. Carter. If there's one thing I don't need—from you or anyone else—it's a shoulder to cry on. And now, for the last time, the film."

"Sure. And thanks for the answers," I retorted, "if not the memories."

"The film."

"Right. It's in my shoe. I got the idea from an old James Bond movie. Hollow heel and all that." I bent down and reached for one of my loafers. There was no sand to throw in her eyes, so I took off the shoe and straightened up again.

"Drop it," she said.

I did, letting the loafer slip from my fingers.

"Now shove it over with your foot."

"It'll be my pleasure," I said. My foot slid forward, but not the way she'd ordered. Instead, I drew my leg up, my knee as close to my chest as possible. Then, within the space of a breath and with a snap that sounded like dozens of knuckles cracking simultaneously, I delivered a front kick, straight out. The thrust was horizontal and Kate squeezed the trigger. The bullet droned past the side of my head like a momentary swarm of bees. I sent my foot lashing out a second time, only to have the kick blocked with an inner forearm blow.

So they've taught her how to defend herself, I thought, not all that surprised that she seemed to have some kind of rudimentary knowledge of karate. But her knowledge of the martial arts didn't concern me nearly as much as her Snub Barrel Sentinel. She didn't hesitate to squeeze the trigger once again.

It jammed.

No doubt Wilhelmina had been responsible for that, when she'd nicked the barrel some fifteen or twenty minutes earlier. Instead of dropping the revolver, Kate turned and fled down the stairs at the end of the narrow passage. I shoved my foot into my shoe, grabbed Wilhelmina, and raced after her.

The light grew dim the moment I passed from the terrace to the stone-walled passage. I could hear her retreating footfalls as I started down the winding steps, taking them as quickly as I could. If she got to the Jeep before I did, I didn't stand a chance in the world. I saw the entire scenario unfurling before me: Kate in the Jeep hurrying back to Pagan; Kate telling the authorities I was the man responsible for the robbery on the train, responsible too for murdering a Burmese citizen, trying to murder her, as well.

I couldn't let that happen.

She was still Mr. X, still an adversary, an opponent, a dangerous enemy. If the security of the free world didn't depend on stopping her, internal U.S. security sure as hell did. I reached the bottom of the stairs, darted down the main corridor and hit the second stairway with all the stops pulled out. Her running footsteps echoed loudly. I chased after her, down the second and narrow set of stone steps until I was once again on the first level of the Manaha.

The three statues of Buddha stared back at me. I eased my index finger down against Wilhelmina's trigger, ready to give her the opportunity to prove herself, all over again. Silence—thick, impalpable—followed me across the dust covered floor. Kate could be hiding just about anywhere. I didn't want to make a run for the Jeep until I knew she wouldn't pump lead into my back, severing my

spinal cord and my spirit from my flesh, all at the same
time.

So I was, of necessity, as cautious and wary as I could
possibly be. I took one step forward, searching the
shadows for any sign of life, movement. A loud creak like
an old door swinging shut on rusty hinges, suddenly broke
above the stillness. I jerked my head to the side, just
as the standing Buddha with the red beestung lips toppled
forward off its pedestal. It crashed to the floor as I threw
myself back, narrowly avoiding being crushed by the mas-
sive clay figure. It split into three pieces, while behind its
architectural niche there came back to me the menacing
flash of gun metal, nickel plate, and iceberg-blue.

The metal and nickel plate belonged to the .357 Magnum. The frigid iceberg-blue belonged to Kate. Her eyes
glinted in the dim light, cold and crystalline. When she
spoke, it was the voice of a computer, impervious to reason, incapable of emotion. "It's the end of the Burma
Road, Nick, the end of Killmaster N3."

She shot and missed.

I shot, and didn't.

EPILOGUE

DAY SEVEN—Dacca, City of a Thousand Mosques.

It was the end of the Burma Road, just as Kate Holmes had promised.

From Paletwa to Cox's Bazar, to Chittagong and then Dacca, the capital of Bangladesh. I had a suite at the Intercontinental with hot and cold running water, air-conditioning—every Western amenity that money could buy. I had a clean bandage on my arm and a layer of fresh scar tissue covering the bullet wound I'd taken back in Pagan. I had a fresh set of clothes on my back and a pain in my chest that would probably take quite some time to get over. It wasn't organic, physiological, or pathological. But if I hadn't pulled the trigger . . .

"The U.S. Embassy," I told the driver who waited right outside the hotel, his bicycle rickshaw as spotless as his starched and flowing white pants, his *kirta* and Moslem cap. I wasn't in any mood to haggle over a rate, so I nodded my head when he came up with a figure and climbed aboard.

We drove around oxcarts and bicyclists, steered clear of the community of cardboard shacks and starving pariahs. I had a pocketful of *rupees* and a pain in my chest. We drove past streets crowded with stalls, sellers sitting squat and tightly compact upon the sidewalk, dusting their inventory with brown feather dusters. The tips of their rubber go-betweens were pointy, and the rows of goods—religious pictures with strange iconographies, rubber and leather sandals, glittering glass and plastic bracelets, penknives with half a dozen assorted blades—were laid out neatly on grass mats that covered the pavement. Small black-haired children ran alongside the pedicab. Dressed in rags, they screamed, *"Bakshish, bakshish"* into the air that smelled of peanuts, curry, and starvation.

I'd traded U San's Jeep for safe passage into Bangladesh, bribing the border guards I was forced to deal with when I reached Paletwa. The ride through the Chin Hills took the two days U San had said it would, and the roads ranged from bad to nonexistent.

Nothing and no one was going to convince me that they hadn't worked Kate over, hadn't done a job on her head. No one was going to make me believe she'd walked into their embassy in Stockholm with a smile in her eyes and the Chairman's wisdom on her lips.

"You wish for me to wait, *sahib?*" the driver asked when he pulled up in front of the embassy compound.

"No, I don't think so. I just might walk back," I said.

"Walk back? Is dangerous. Many peoples will ask for money."

When I didn't answer he shrugged his shoulders and extended his hand. The *rupees* dropped into his sweaty palm. I showed my I.D. to the guard stationed outside the gates, then stepped inside the compound and headed down a long gravel drive which led up to the steps of the embassy.

The microfilm was due to fly out that night, safe inside the ambassador's diplomatic pouch. Hawk would be waiting for it at the airport, while I was scheduled to return to Washington in two days' time. All the loose ends had been tied up but one.

I was met at the door by the ambassador's special assistant, a dour young man in an equally dour pinstripe suit. He didn't epitomize the new breed of responsive career diplomats, but he wasn't completely ineffectual, either.

"How are you feeling today, Mr. Carter?" he asked, no doubt more concerned about the social graces than my state of health.

"Tired," I said, though my fatigue was much more mental than physical. "Is the microfiche reader set up?"

"Right this way."

I followed him through the lobby, then down one bureaucratic corridor after another. Typewriters rattled furiously. Phones rang. The unending hum of the air-conditioning unit vibrated all around me. "Busy operation you've got here," I said.

"Always has been . . . always will be."

At last he opened a door at the end of one of the corridors. It was a small square room, empty save for a chair and a wooden desk upon which the microreader had been set up.

"I'll be right outside if you need me," he said, stepping back to let me enter. "Know how to work that thing?"

I nodded my head. "I think I can figure it out."

The door closed behind him and I sat down at the desk, took off my watch, and unscrewed the back of the Rolex's stainless steel case. Gingerly, I removed the roll of microfilm and reassembled the watchcase.

Five minutes later the last loose end had been tied with a double knot. There it was, staring me right in the eye, absolute and irrefutable. It wasn't difficult translating from Chinese to English:

HOLMES, KATHERINE aka Hollis, Carolyn aka Carlton, Helene. b.1951, Kenosha, Wisconsin, U.S.A. Last known address: 608 East 84 Street, New York City. Observations: Theatrical training (3 yrs. People's Theater), archaeological background, Weathermen (2 yrs.). Excellent small arms, good martial arts. Fluent Chinese, Russian, German . . .

I thought of Sam Spade, Dash Hammett's great fictional creation. I thought of how he'd once said, "I won't play the sap for you."

The pain in my chest had already begun to fade. In fact, I hardly felt any pain at all.

TIME CLOCK OF DEATH   Nick Carter
The U.S. and Russia in a nuclear showdown. Killmaster races to stop the inevitable slaughter.   AQ1370—$1.25

STRIKE FORCE TERROR   Nick Carter
Nick Carter infiltrates Russia's most notorious slave labor camp to thwart an electrifying kidnap attempt.   AQ1298—$1.25

SEVEN AGAINST GREECE   Nick Carter
Seven powerful men form an alliance of hate against the free world.   AQ1393—$1.25

SIX BLOODY SUMMER DAYS   Nick Carter
A billion-dollar blackmail plot is backed by deadly nuclear artillery. Millions will die if Killmaster doesn't get to the extortionists in time!   AQ1449—$1.25

14 SECONDS TO HELL   Nick Carter
World destruction is just seconds away as Carter battles his way deep inside Red China.   AQ1448—$1.25

THE ULTIMATE CODE   Nick Carter
N3 on the trail of a vital decoding machine—and in the middle of an international espionage coup that threatens world disaster!   AQ1486—$1.25

THE ARAB PLAGUE   Nick Carter
Arab slave traders plot to sabotage the hair-trigger machinery of international politics!   AQ1513—$1.25

ASSIGNMENT: INTERCEPT   Nick Carter
Carter tracks a Chinese scientist armed with a diabolical weapon that can trigger flaming death anywere in the world!   AQ1512—$1.25

THE GREEN WOLF CONNECTION   Nick Carter
It's Killmaster alone against a daring corporate conspiracy to seize world power—starting with the oil-rich Middle East!   AQ1546—$1.25

THE LIVING DEATH   Nick Carter
The best minds in the Free World are being destroyed by a hideous poison. Killmaster must find the lone-wolf infiltrator!   AQ1561—$1.25

USE HANDY, MONEY-SAVING ORDER FORM ON BACK PAGE

DEATH MESSAGE: OIL 74-2 **Nick Carter**

An obscure coded message holds the key to a lethal outbreak of sabotage that is destroying America's vital oil supply lines!

AQ1559—$1.25

RUSH YOUR ORDER TODAY!

AWARD BOOKS,
350 Kennedy Drive, Hauppauge, N.Y. 11788

Please send me the books checked below by number:

☐ AY1424 $1.95		☐ AQ1455 $1.25	
☐ AQ1439 $1.25		☐ AN1133 95¢	
☐ AQ1414 $1.25		☐ AQ1493 $1.25	
☐ AQ1400 $1.25		☐ AQ1490 $1.25	
☐ AQ1354 $1.25		☐ AQ1502 $1.25	
☐ AQ1547 $1.25		☐ AQ1501 $1.25	
☐ AQ1297 $1.25		☐ AQ1479 $1.25	
☐ AQ1474 $1.25		☐ AN1227 95¢	
☐ AQ1460 $1.25		☐ AQ1388 $1.25	
☐ AQ1356 $1.25		☐ AN1270 95¢	
☐ AQ1331 $1.25		☐ AQ1370 $1.25	
☐ AQ1329 $1.25		☐ AQ1298 $1.25	
☐ AQ1333 $1.25		☐ AQ1393 $1.25	
☐ AQ1415 $1.25		☐ AQ1449 $1.25	
☐ AQ1440 $1.25		☐ AQ1448 $1.25	
☐ AQ1401 $1.25		☐ AQ1486 $1.25	
☐ AQ1387 $1.25		☐ AQ1513 $1.25	
☐ AN1178 95¢		☐ AQ1512 $1.25	
☐ AQ1477 $1.25		☐ AQ1546 $1.25	
☐ AQ1456 $1.25		☐ AQ1561 $1.25	
☐ AQ1454 $1.25		☐ AQ1559 $1.25	

I am enclosing $_____

SAVE $ $ $ 5 books or more, deduct 10% discount
DISCOUNT   8 books or more, deduct 15% discount
PLAN   10 books or more, deduct 20% discount

Name_____

Address_____

City_____State_____Zip_____

Add 25¢ for postage and handling for one book, 35¢ for two or three books. We pay postage on all orders of four books or more. Send remittance in U.S. or Canadian funds. Sorry, no C.O.D.s.